ILLEGAL

For Jackie, Finn and Seán. —EC

For Viv, Lexie and Fisher. —AD

For Paola, always. —GR

ILLEGAL

EOIN COLFER
ANDREW DONKIN

ART BY GIOVANNI RIGANO

LETTERING BY CHRIS DICKEY

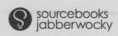
sourcebooks
jabberwocky

Copyright © 2018 by Eoin Colfer and Andrew Donkin
Cover and internal illustrations © Giovanni Rigano
Cover design © 2018 by Travis Hasenour/Sourcebooks, Inc.
Written by Eoin Colfer and Andrew Donkin
Lettering by Chris Dickey

Sourcebooks and the colophon are registered trademarks of Sourcebooks, Inc.

Quotation on page v: Remarks on immigration by Elie Wiesel. Copyright © Elie
Wiesel. Reprinted by permission of Georges Borchardt, Inc., on behalf of the Estate of
Elie Wiesel.

Published by Sourcebooks Jabberwocky, an imprint of Sourcebooks, Inc.
P.O. Box 4410, Naperville, Illinois 60567-4410
(630) 961-3900
Fax: (630) 961-2168
sourcebooks.com

Originally published in 2017 in Great Britain by Hodder Children's Books, an imprint
of Hachette Children's Group, part of Hodder and Stoughton.

Library of Congress Cataloging-in-Publication Data is on file with the publisher.

Source of Production: RR Donnelley Asia Printing Solutions Limited
Date of Production: March 2018
Run Number: 5011522

Printed and bound in China.
RRD 10 9 8 7 6 5 4 3 2 1

You, who are so-called illegal aliens, must know that no human being is illegal. That is a contradiction in terms. Human beings can be beautiful or more beautiful, they can be fat or skinny, they can be right or wrong, but illegal? How can a human being be illegal?

—Elie Wiesel
Nobel Laureate and
Holocaust survivor

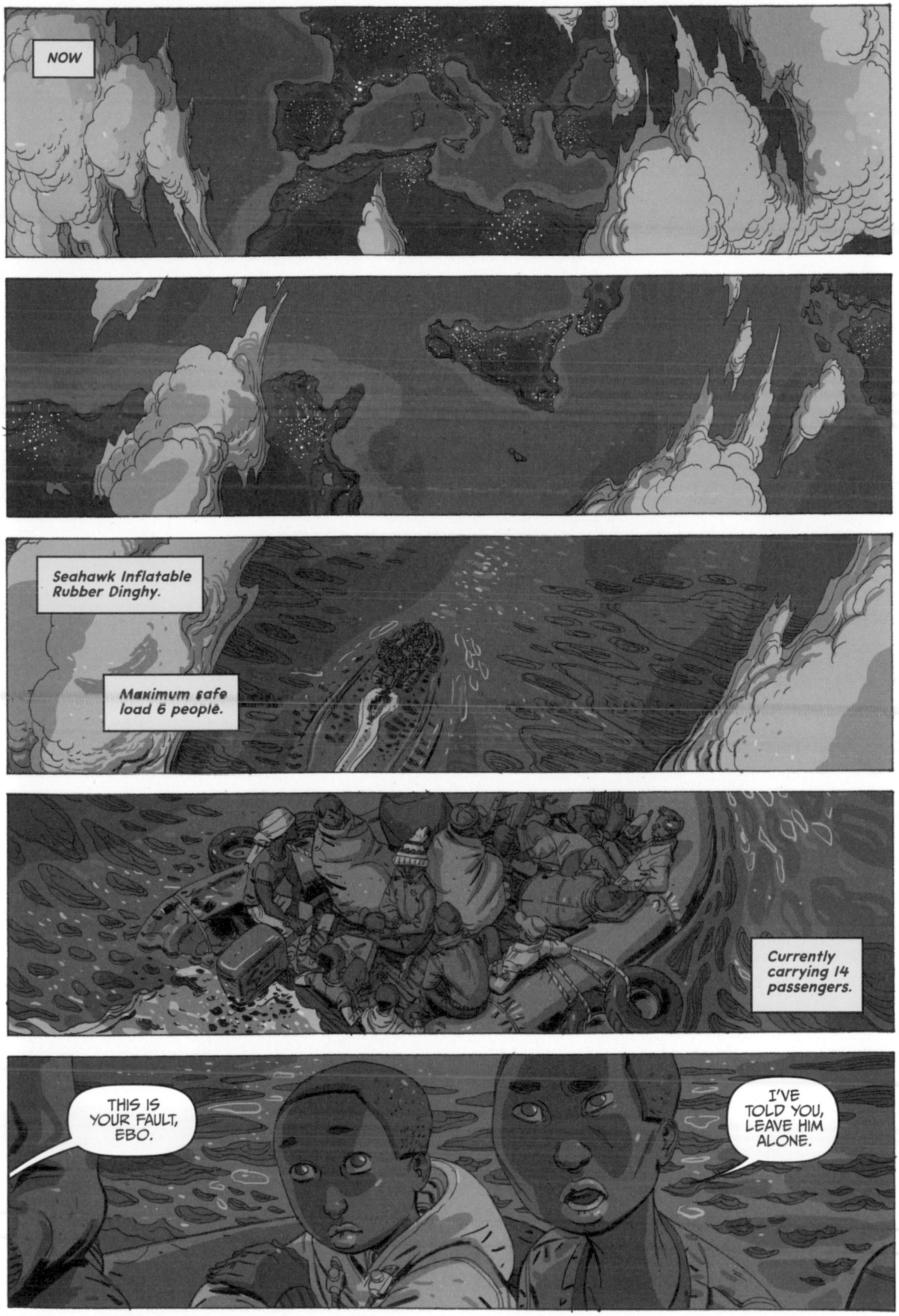
NOW
Seahawk Inflatable Rubber Dinghy.
Maximum safe load 6 people.
Currently carrying 14 passengers.
THIS IS YOUR FAULT, EBO.
I'VE TOLD YOU, LEAVE HIM ALONE.

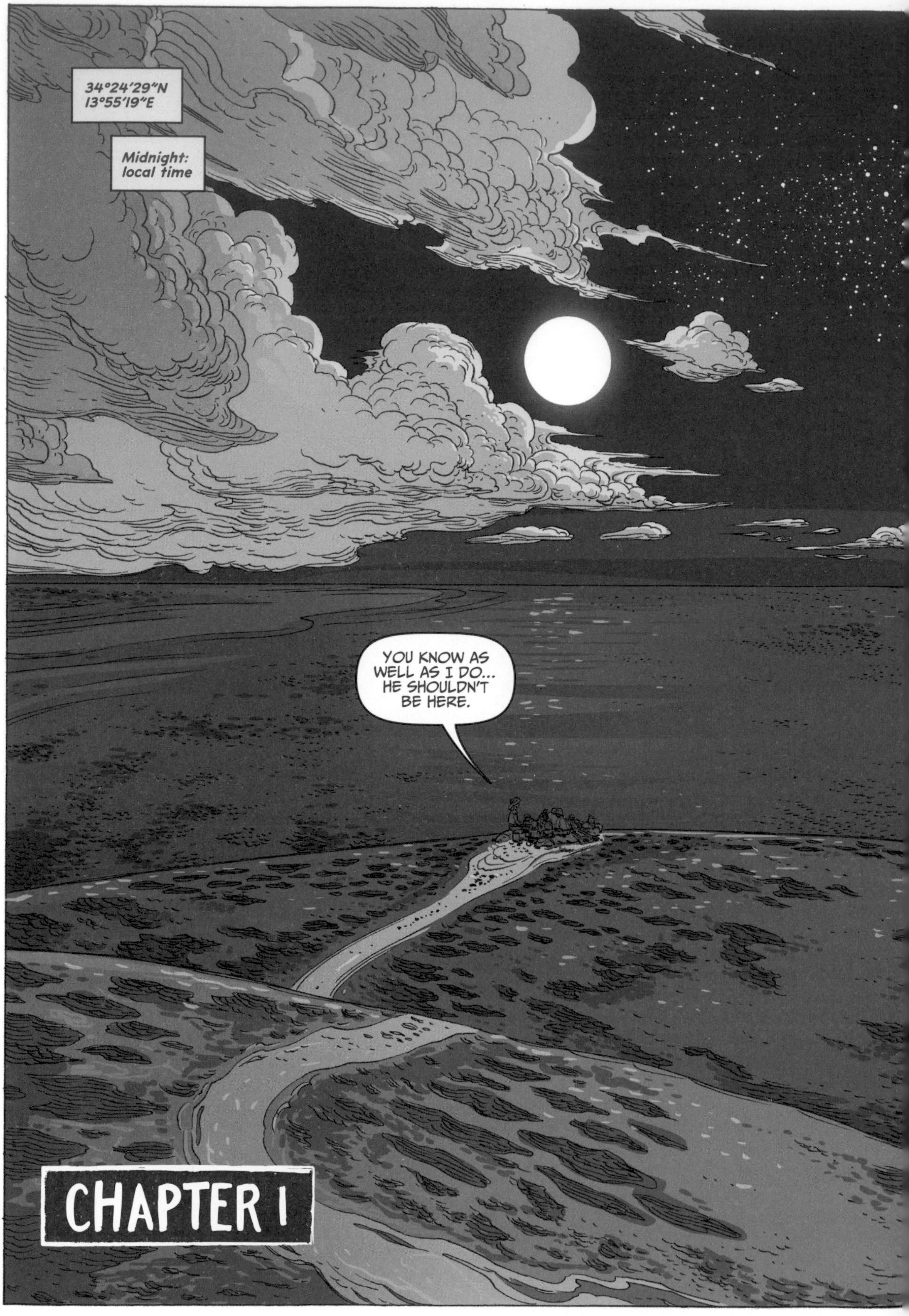
34°24'29"N
13°55'19"E
Midnight:
local time
YOU KNOW AS WELL AS I DO... HE SHOULDN'T BE HERE.
CHAPTER 1

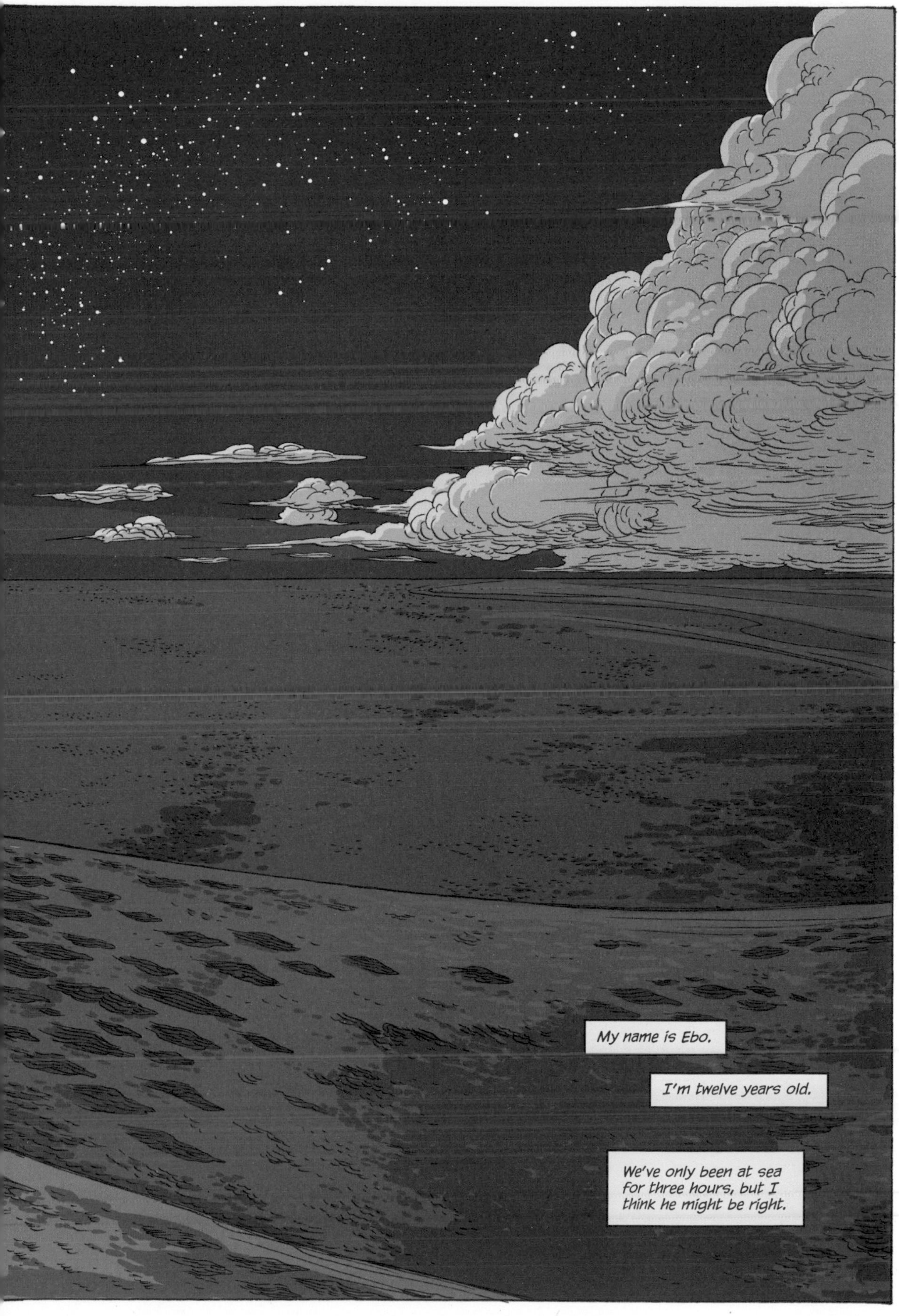
My name is Ebo.
I'm twelve years old.
We've only been at sea for three hours, but I think he might be right.

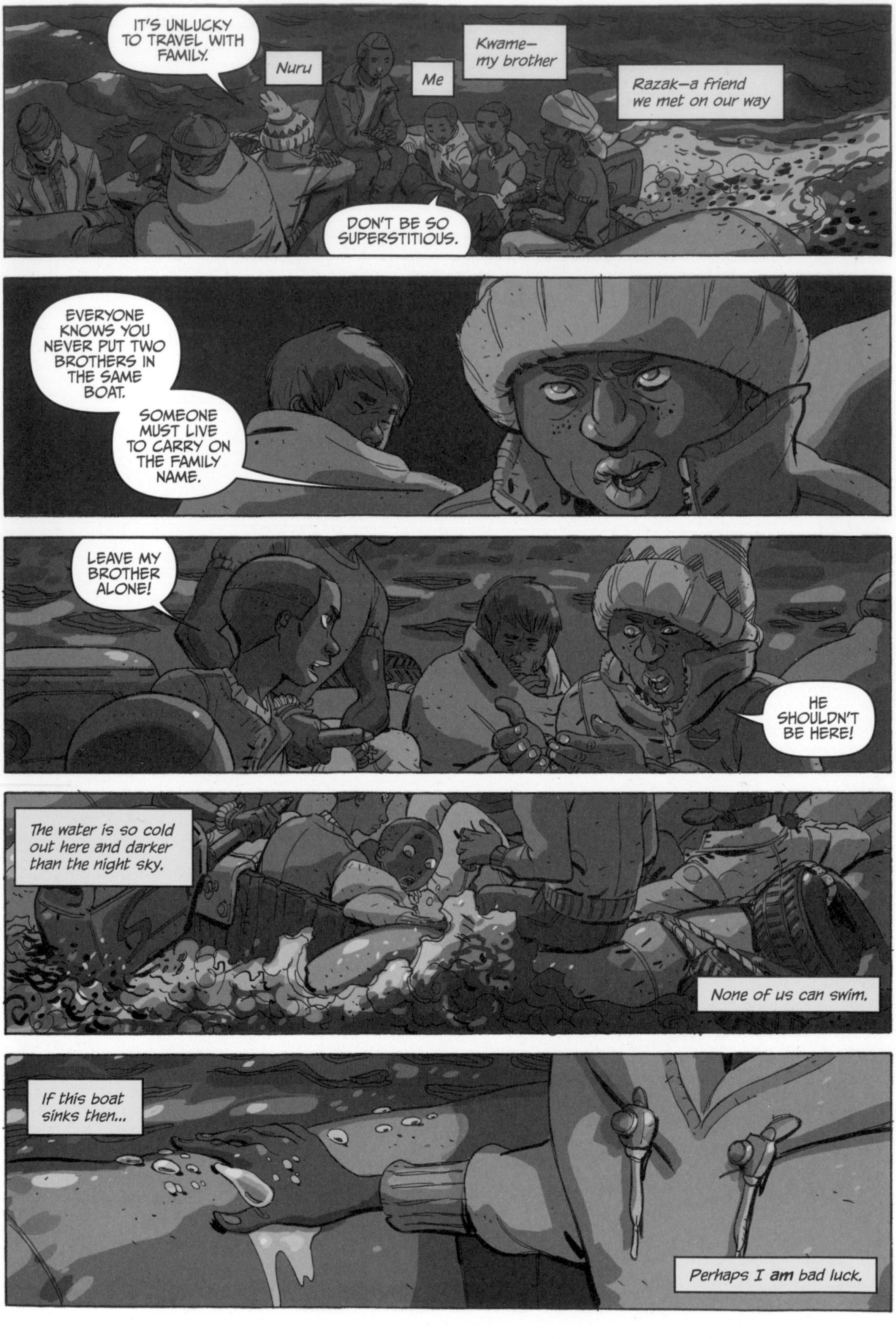
IT'S UNLUCKY TO TRAVEL WITH FAMILY.
Nuru
Me
Kwame—my brother
Razak—a friend we met on our way
DON'T BE SO SUPERSTITIOUS.
EVERYONE KNOWS YOU NEVER PUT TWO BROTHERS IN THE SAME BOAT.
SOMEONE MUST LIVE TO CARRY ON THE FAMILY NAME.
LEAVE MY BROTHER ALONE!
HE SHOULDN'T BE HERE!
The water is so cold out here and darker than the night sky.
None of us can swim.
If this boat sinks then...
Perhaps I **am** bad luck.

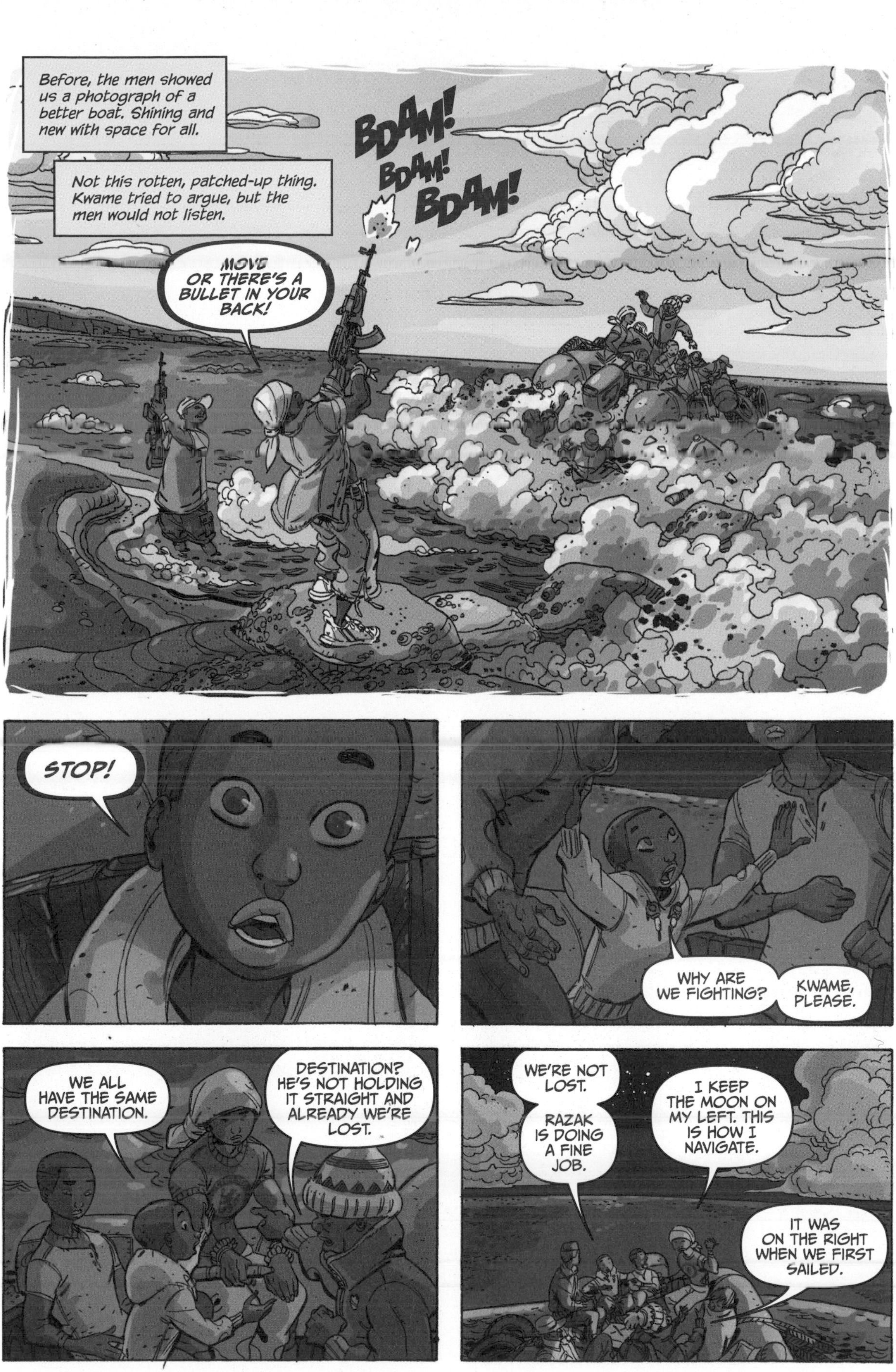

Before, the men showed us a photograph of a better boat. Shining and new with space for all.
Not this rotten, patched-up thing. Kwame tried to argue, but the men would not listen.
BDAM! BDAM! BDAM!
MOVE OR THERE'S A BULLET IN YOUR BACK!
STOP!
WHY ARE WE FIGHTING?
KWAME, PLEASE.
WE ALL HAVE THE SAME DESTINATION.
DESTINATION? HE'S NOT HOLDING IT STRAIGHT AND ALREADY WE'RE LOST.
WE'RE NOT LOST.
RAZAK IS DOING A FINE JOB.
I KEEP THE MOON ON MY LEFT. THIS IS HOW I NAVIGATE.
IT WAS ON THE RIGHT WHEN WE FIRST SAILED.

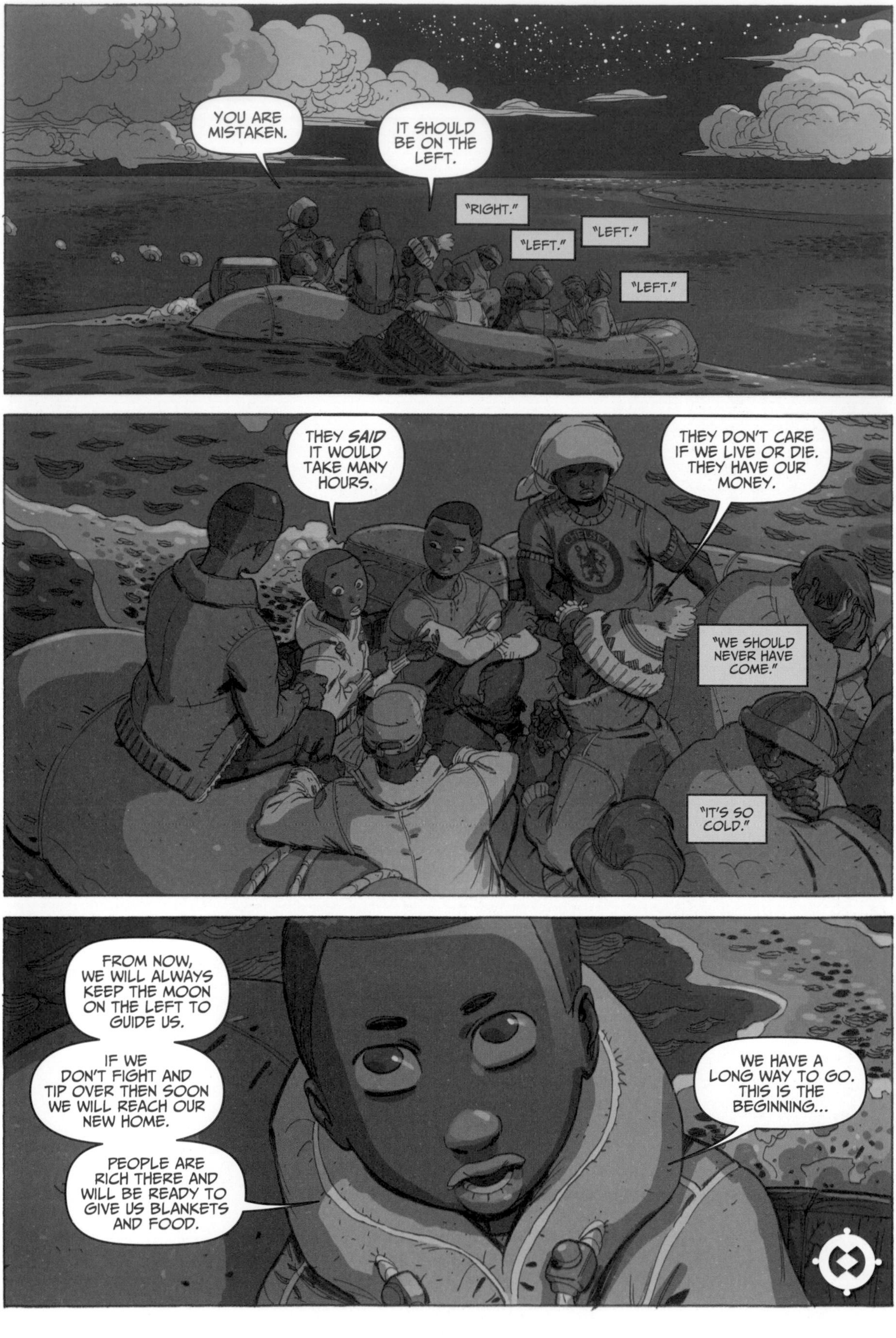
YOU ARE MISTAKEN.
IT SHOULD BE ON THE LEFT.
"RIGHT."
"LEFT."
"LEFT."
"LEFT."
THEY *SAID* IT WOULD TAKE MANY HOURS.
THEY DON'T CARE IF WE LIVE OR DIE. THEY HAVE OUR MONEY.
"WE SHOULD NEVER HAVE COME."
"IT'S SO COLD."
FROM NOW, WE WILL ALWAYS KEEP THE MOON ON THE LEFT TO GUIDE US.
IF WE DON'T FIGHT AND TIP OVER THEN SOON WE WILL REACH OUR NEW HOME.
PEOPLE ARE RICH THERE AND WILL BE READY TO GIVE US BLANKETS AND FOOD.
WE HAVE A LONG WAY TO GO. THIS IS THE BEGINNING...

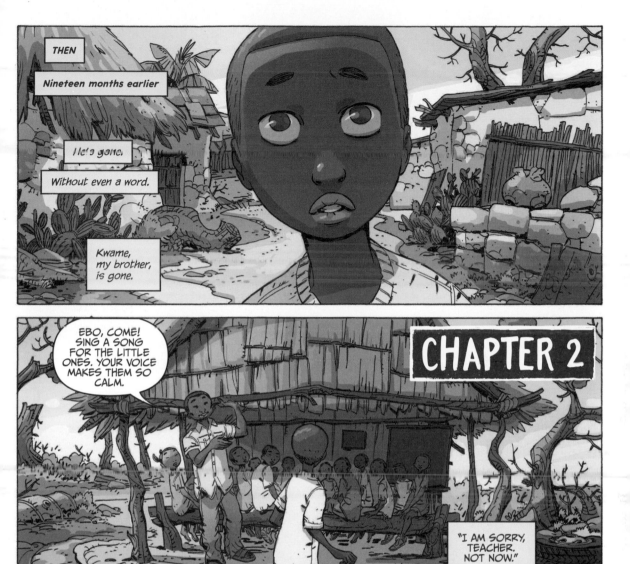

THEN

Nineteen months earlier

He's gone.

Without even a word.

Kwame, my brother, is gone.

EBO, COME! SING A SONG FOR THE LITTLE ONES. YOUR VOICE MAKES THEM SO CALM.

CHAPTER 2

"I AM SORRY, TEACHER. NOT NOW."

Perhaps Kwame is still in the village.

Market.

Soccer field.

Maybe the old well.

With the other boys.

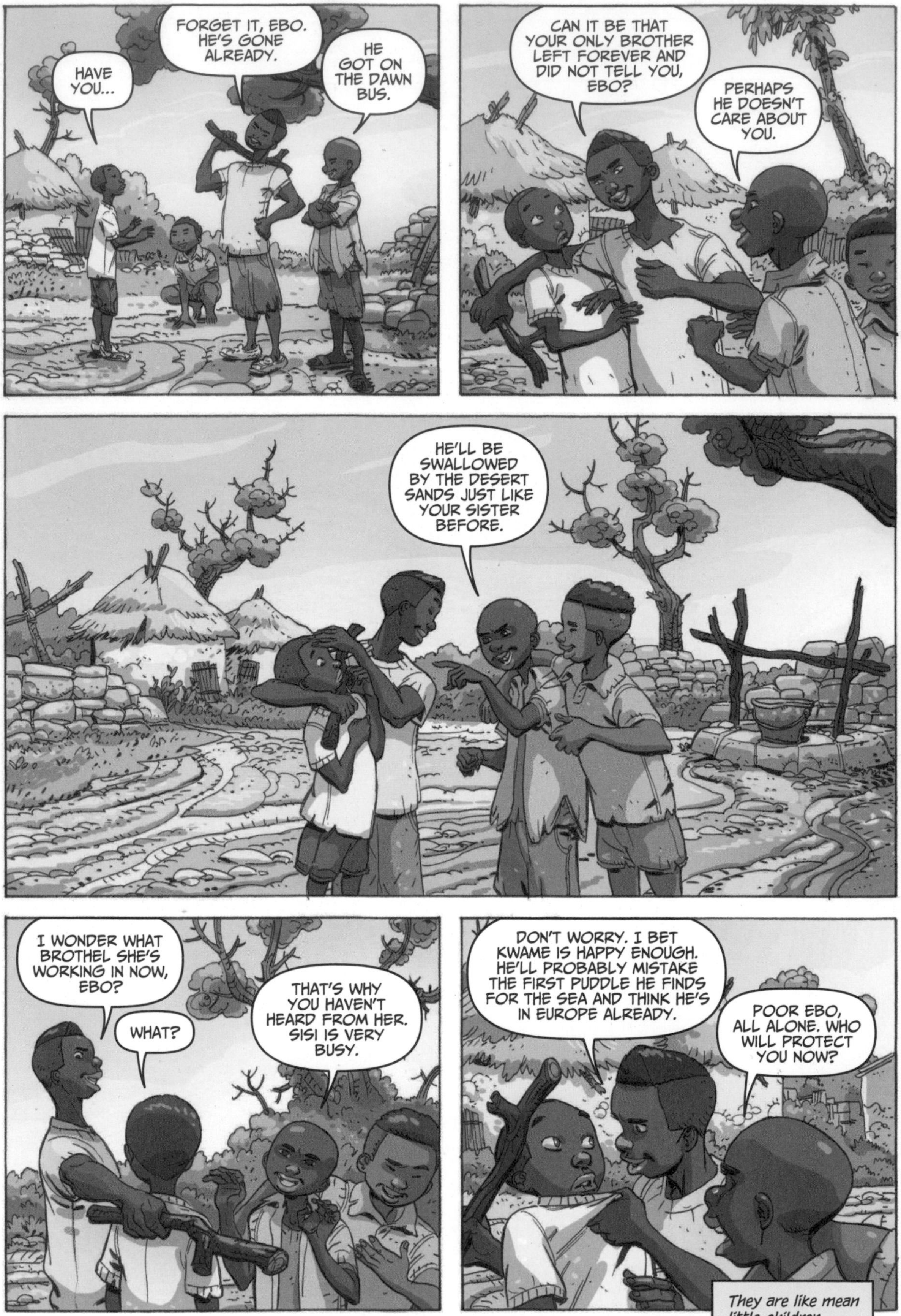
HAVE YOU...
FORGET IT, EBO. HE'S GONE ALREADY.
HE GOT ON THE DAWN BUS.
CAN IT BE THAT YOUR ONLY BROTHER LEFT FOREVER AND DID NOT TELL YOU, EBO?
PERHAPS HE DOESN'T CARE ABOUT YOU.
HE'LL BE SWALLOWED BY THE DESERT SANDS JUST LIKE YOUR SISTER BEFORE.
I WONDER WHAT BROTHEL SHE'S WORKING IN NOW, EBO?
WHAT?
THAT'S WHY YOU HAVEN'T HEARD FROM HER. SISI IS VERY BUSY.
DON'T WORRY. I BET KWAME IS HAPPY ENOUGH. HE'LL PROBABLY MISTAKE THE FIRST PUDDLE HE FINDS FOR THE SEA AND THINK HE'S IN EUROPE ALREADY.
POOR EBO, ALL ALONE. WHO WILL PROTECT YOU NOW?
They are like mean little children.

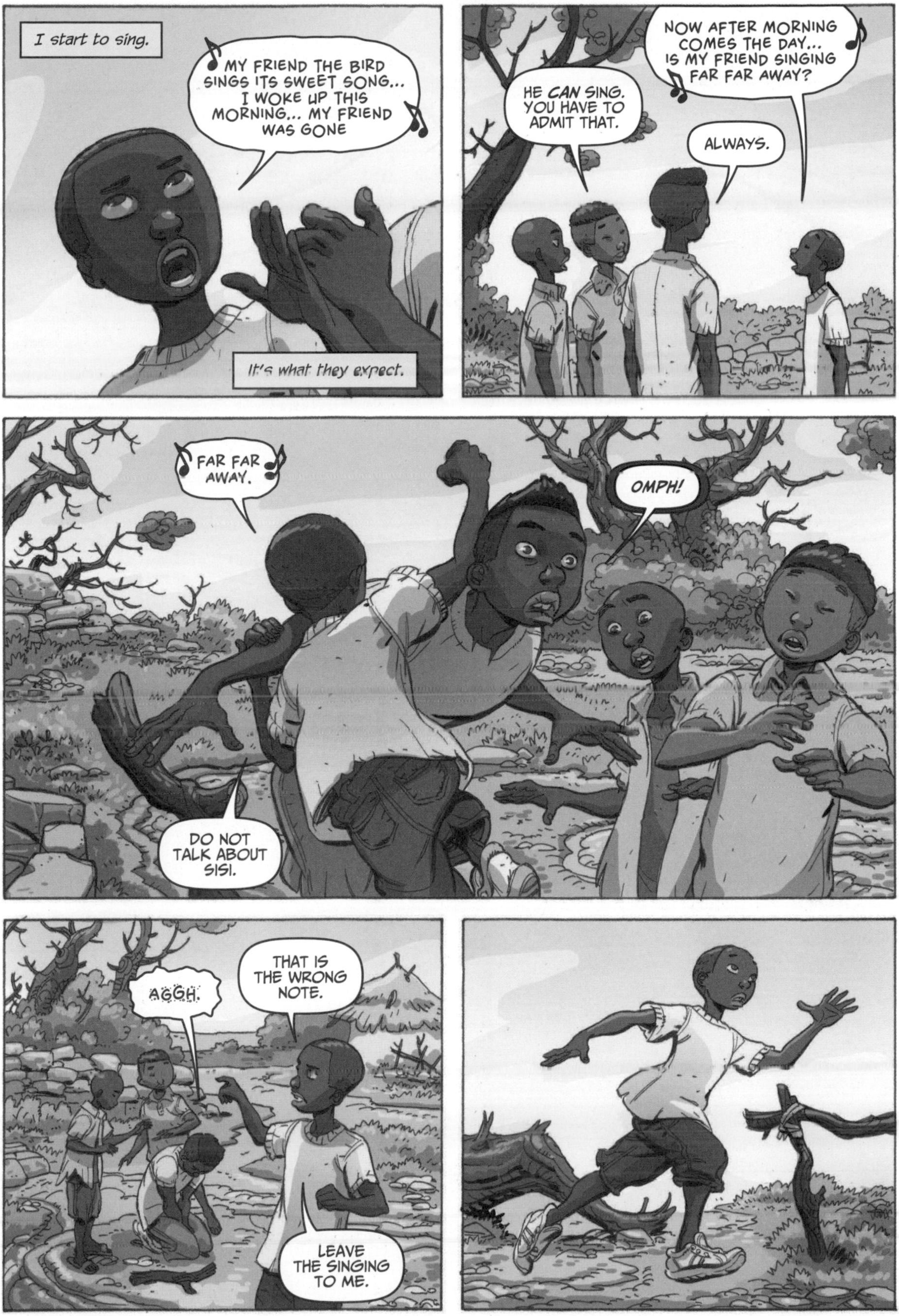
I start to sing.
MY FRIEND THE BIRD SINGS ITS SWEET SONG... I WOKE UP THIS MORNING... MY FRIEND WAS GONE
It's what they expect.
HE CAN SING. YOU HAVE TO ADMIT THAT.
NOW AFTER MORNING COMES THE DAY... IS MY FRIEND SINGING FAR FAR AWAY?
ALWAYS.
FAR FAR AWAY.
OMPH!
DO NOT TALK ABOUT SISI.
AGGH.
THAT IS THE WRONG NOTE.
LEAVE THE SINGING TO ME.

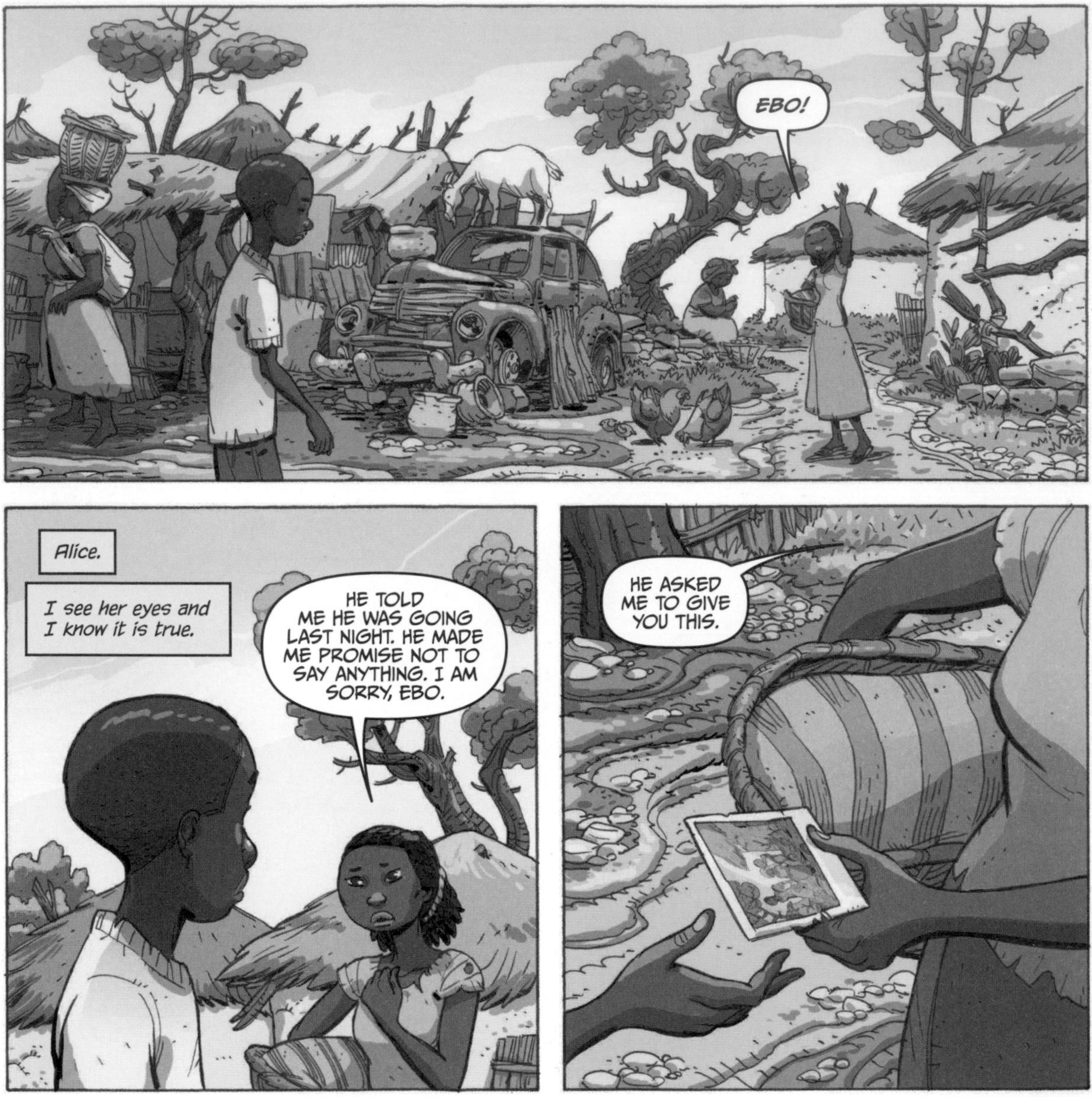
EBO!
Alice.
I see her eyes and I know it is true.
HE TOLD ME HE WAS GOING LAST NIGHT. HE MADE ME PROMISE NOT TO SAY ANYTHING. I AM SORRY, EBO.
HE ASKED ME TO GIVE YOU THIS.
Ebo-
I will go to Europe-
I will find Sisi-
I will send money for you to come later by helicopter-
this is mine to do-
Kwame-

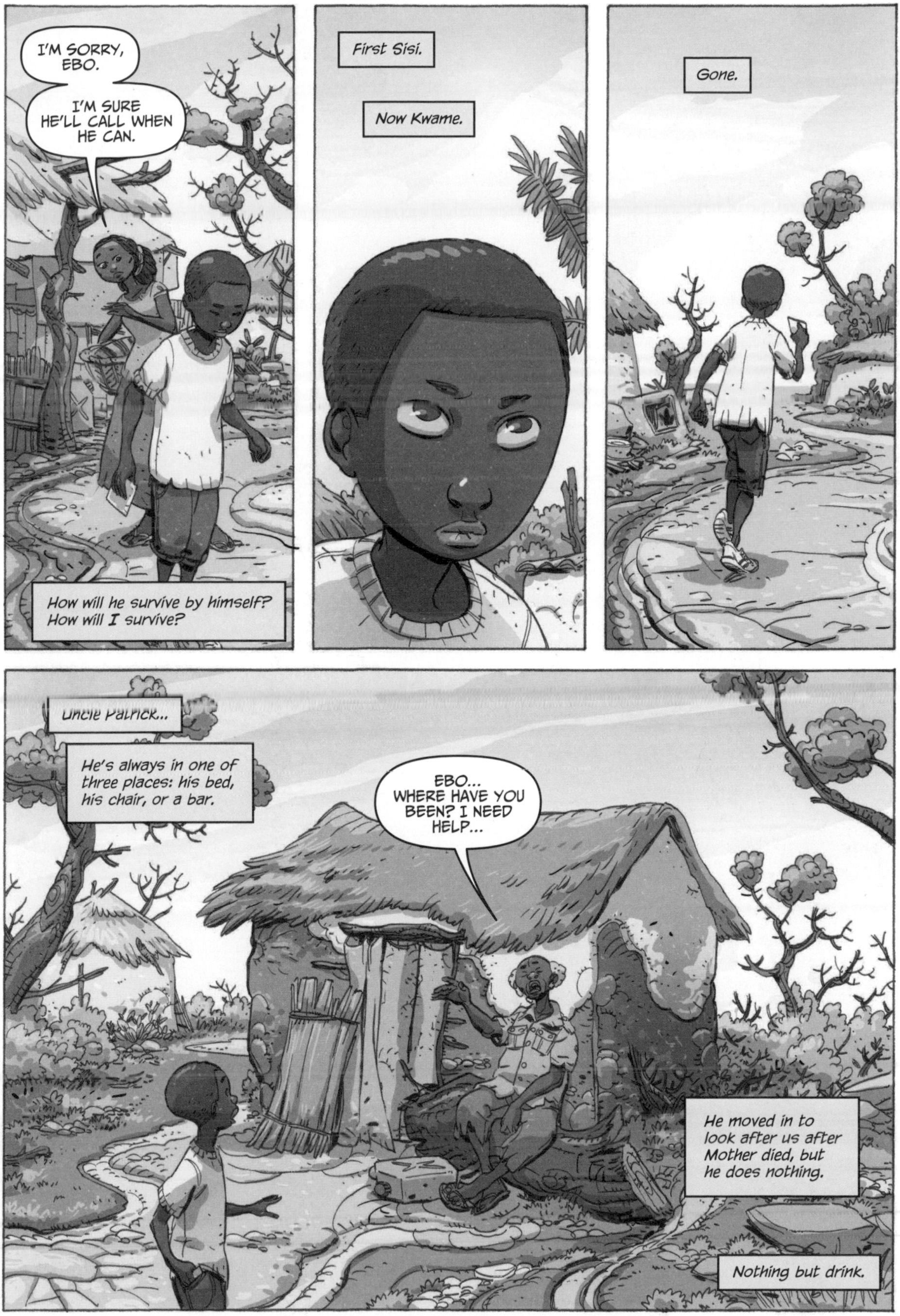
I'M SORRY, EBO.
I'M SURE HE'LL CALL WHEN HE CAN.
How will he survive by himself? How will I survive?
First Sisi.
Now Kwame.
Gone.
Uncle Patrick...
He's always in one of three places: his bed, his chair, or a bar.
EBO... WHERE HAVE YOU BEEN? I NEED HELP...
He moved in to look after us after Mother died, but he does nothing.
Nothing but drink.

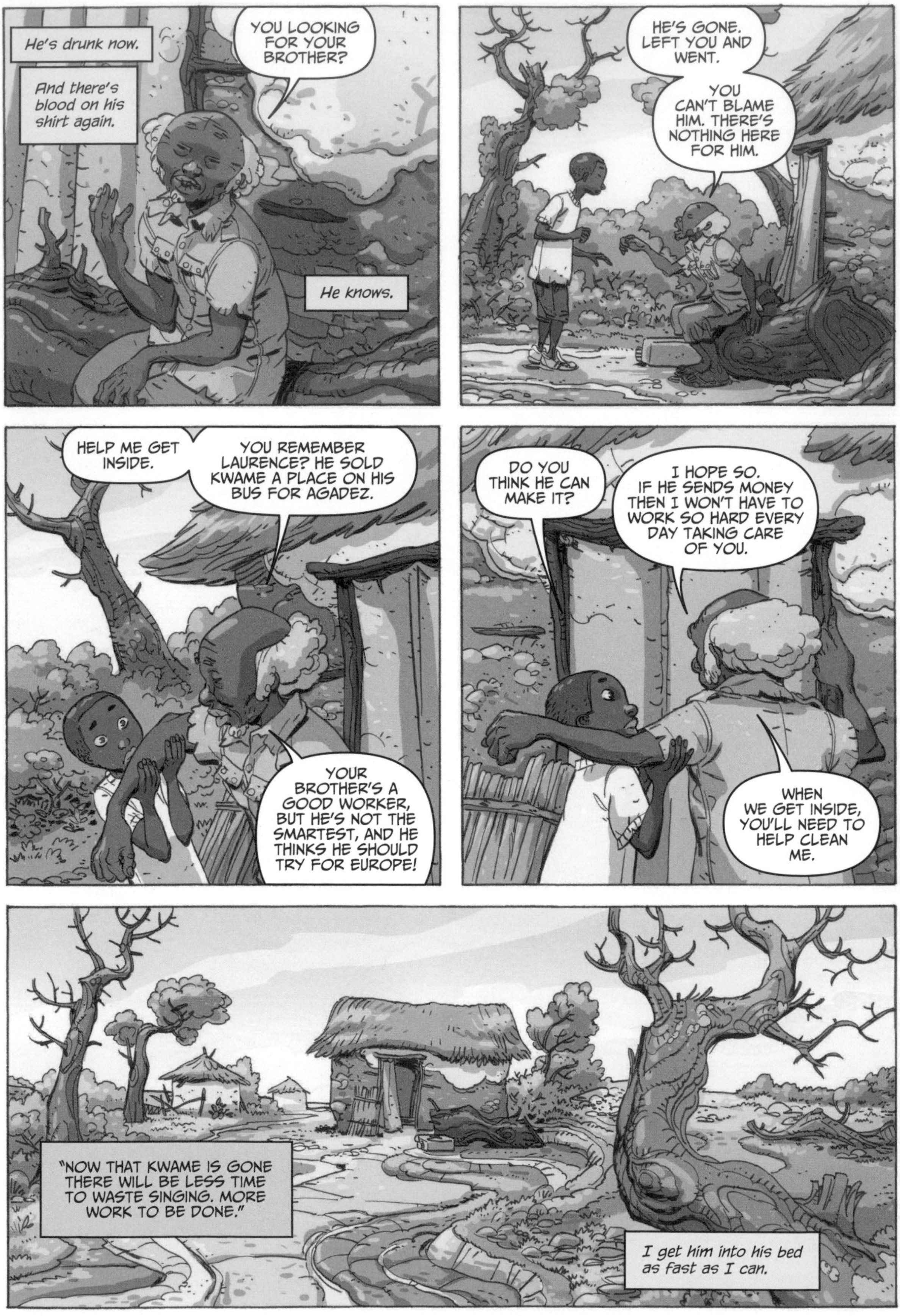

He's drunk now.
And there's blood on his shirt again.
YOU LOOKING FOR YOUR BROTHER?
He knows.
HE'S GONE. LEFT YOU AND WENT.
YOU CAN'T BLAME HIM. THERE'S NOTHING HERE FOR HIM.
HELP ME GET INSIDE.
YOU REMEMBER LAURENCE? HE SOLD KWAME A PLACE ON HIS BUS FOR AGADEZ.
YOUR BROTHER'S A GOOD WORKER, BUT HE'S NOT THE SMARTEST, AND HE THINKS HE SHOULD TRY FOR EUROPE!
DO YOU THINK HE CAN MAKE IT?
I HOPE SO. IF HE SENDS MONEY THEN I WON'T HAVE TO WORK SO HARD EVERY DAY TAKING CARE OF YOU.
WHEN WE GET INSIDE, YOU'LL NEED TO HELP CLEAN ME.
"NOW THAT KWAME IS GONE THERE WILL BE LESS TIME TO WASTE SINGING. MORE WORK TO BE DONE."
I get him into his bed as fast as I can.

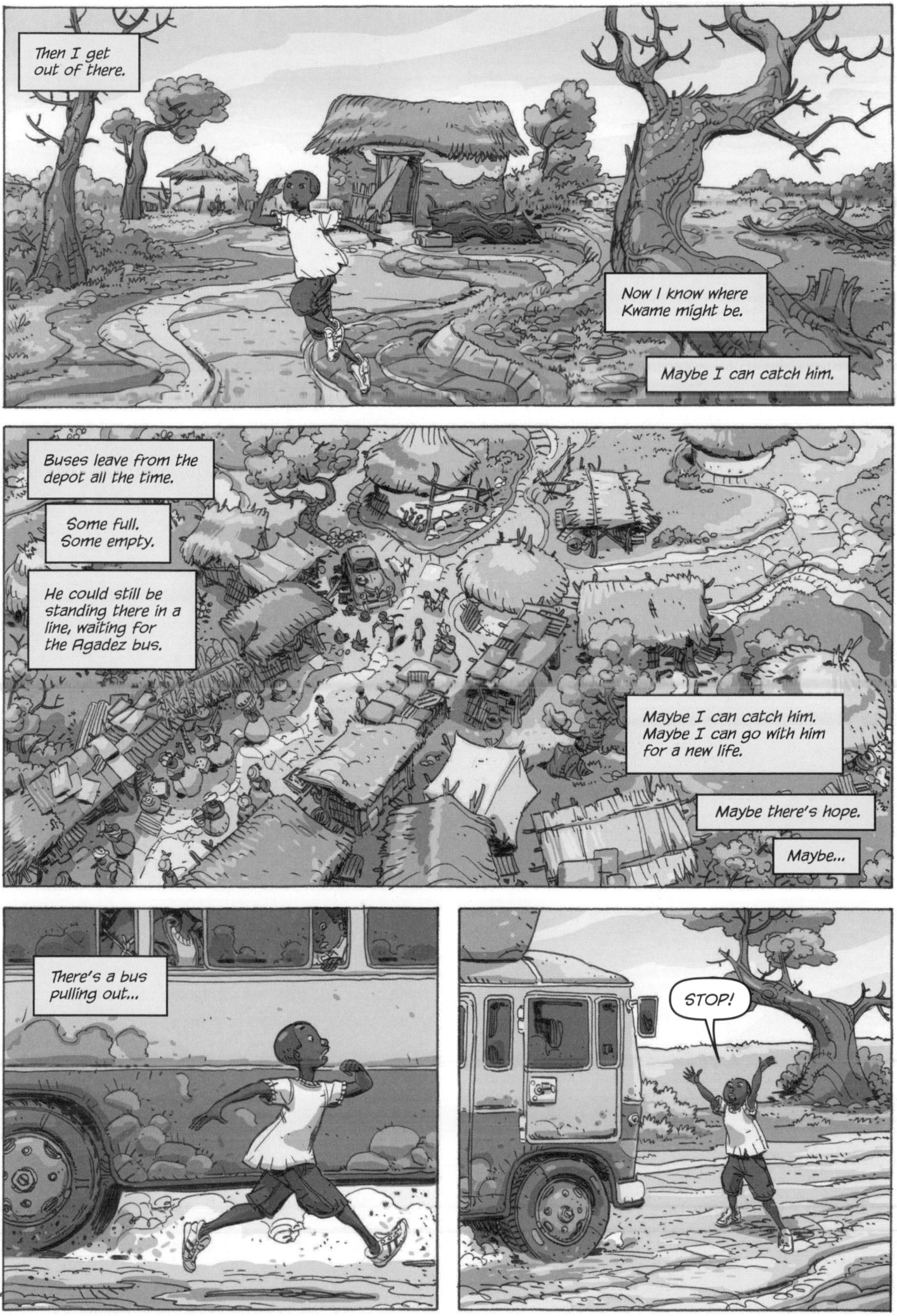
Then I get out of there.
Now I know where Kwame might be.
Maybe I can catch him.
Buses leave from the depot all the time.
Some full. Some empty.
He could still be standing there in a line, waiting for the Agadez bus.
Maybe I can catch him. Maybe I can go with him for a new life.
Maybe there's hope.
Maybe...
There's a bus pulling out...
STOP!

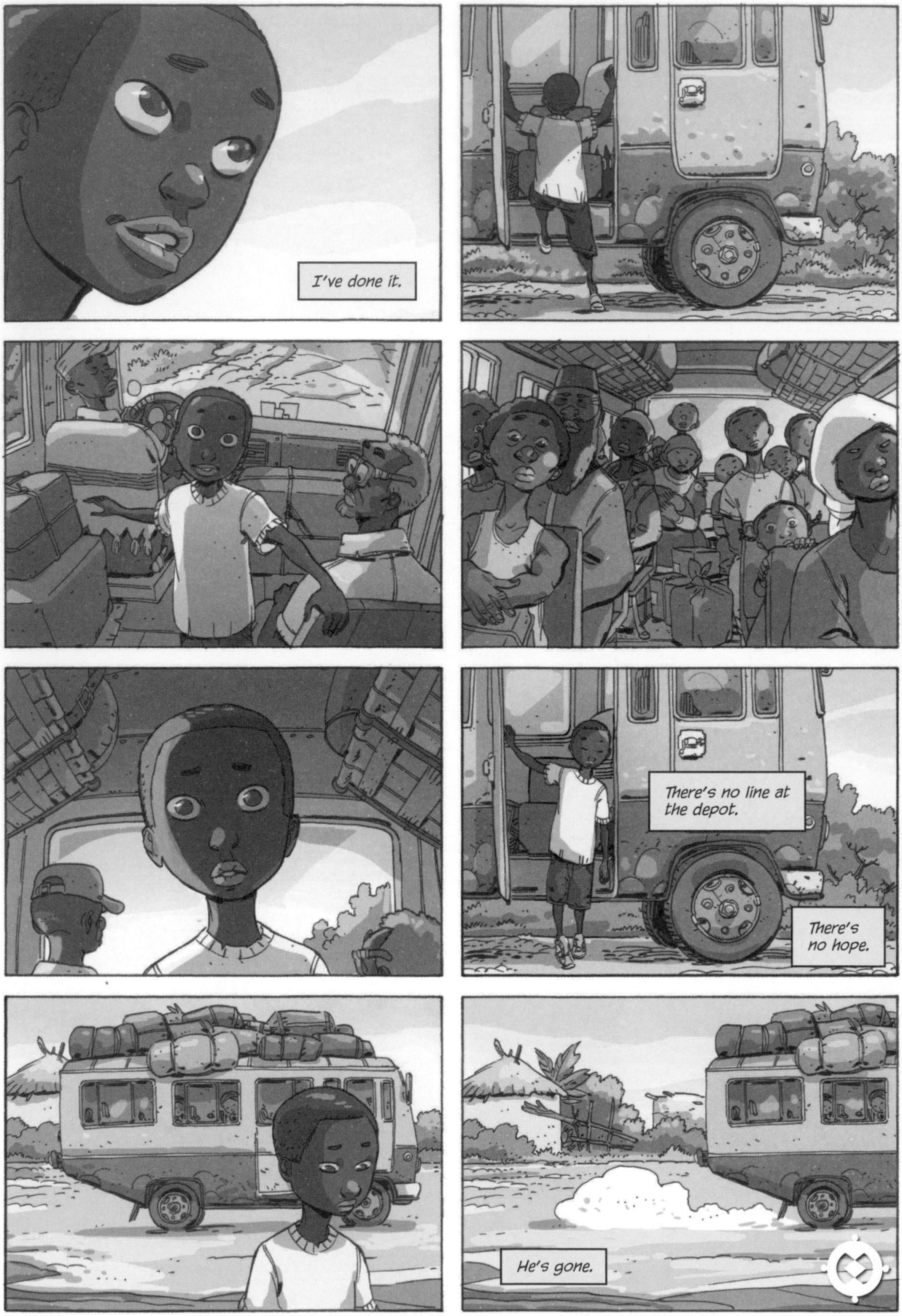
I've done it.
There's no line at the depot.
There's no hope.
He's gone.

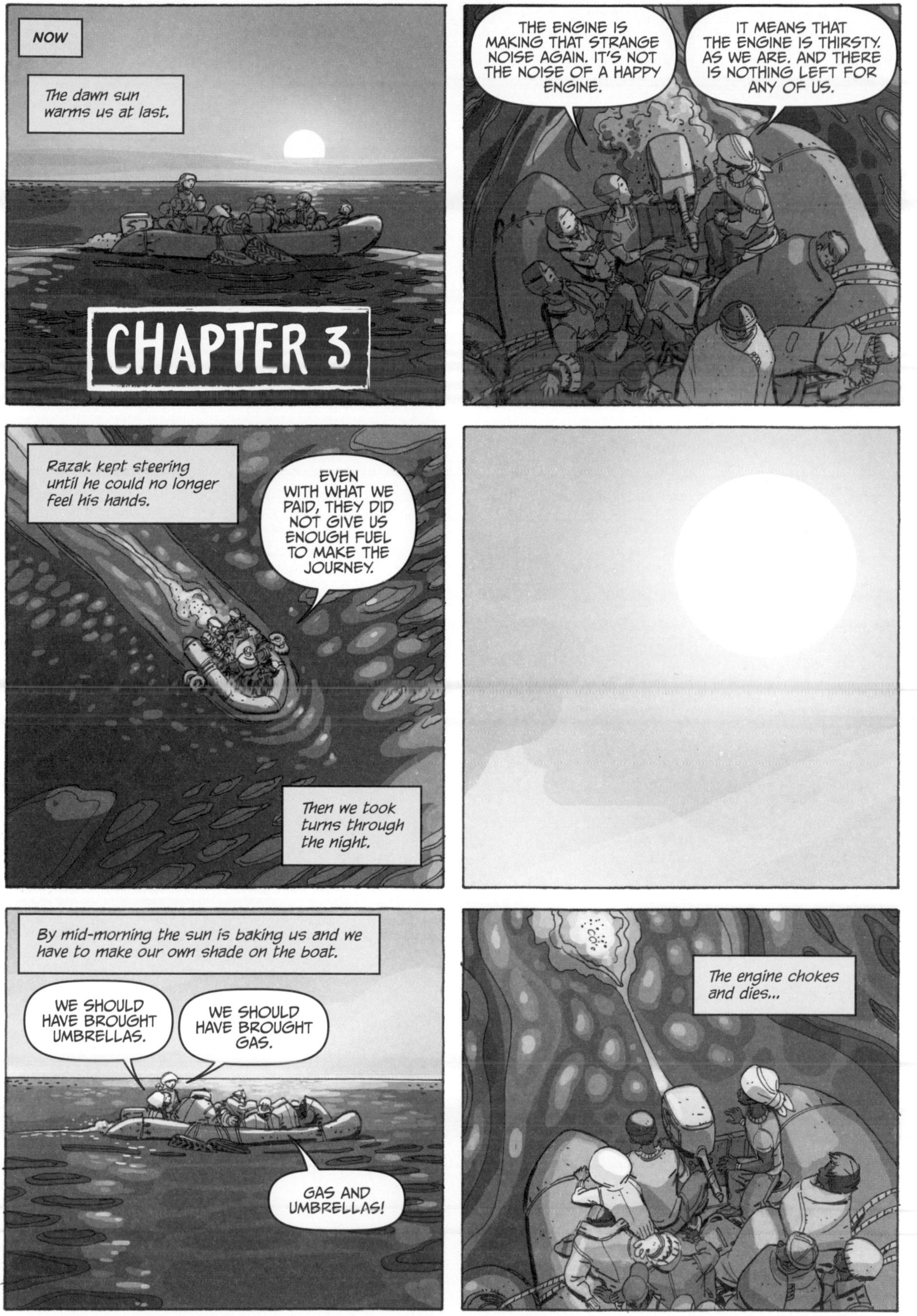
NOW
The dawn sun warms us at last.
CHAPTER 3
THE ENGINE IS MAKING THAT STRANGE NOISE AGAIN. IT'S NOT THE NOISE OF A HAPPY ENGINE.
IT MEANS THAT THE ENGINE IS THIRSTY. AS WE ARE. AND THERE IS NOTHING LEFT FOR ANY OF US.
Razak kept steering until he could no longer feel his hands.
EVEN WITH WHAT WE PAID, THEY DID NOT GIVE US ENOUGH FUEL TO MAKE THE JOURNEY.
Then we took turns through the night.
By mid-morning the sun is baking us and we have to make our own shade on the boat.
WE SHOULD HAVE BROUGHT UMBRELLAS.
WE SHOULD HAVE BROUGHT GAS.
GAS AND UMBRELLAS!
The engine chokes and dies...

16

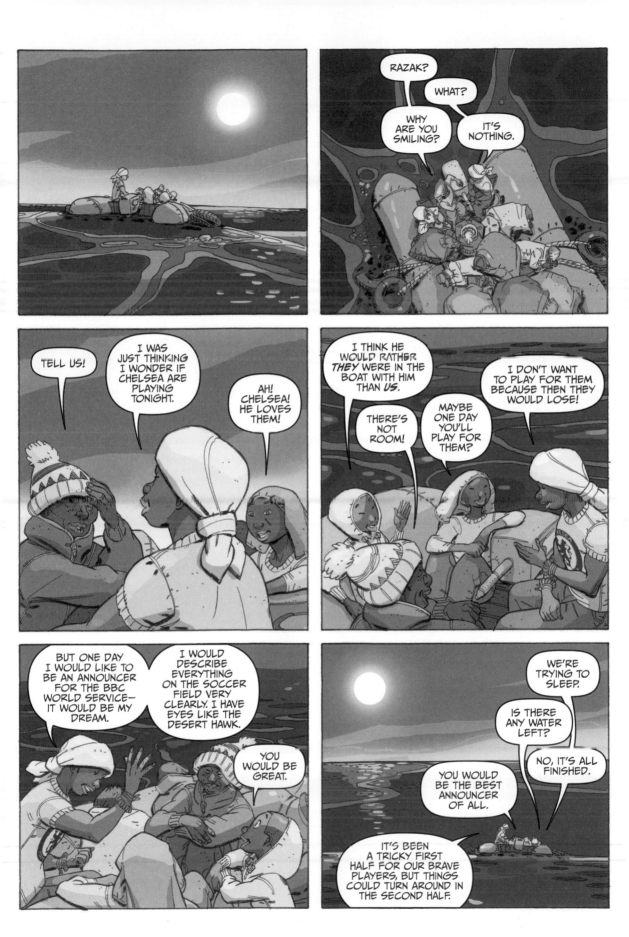

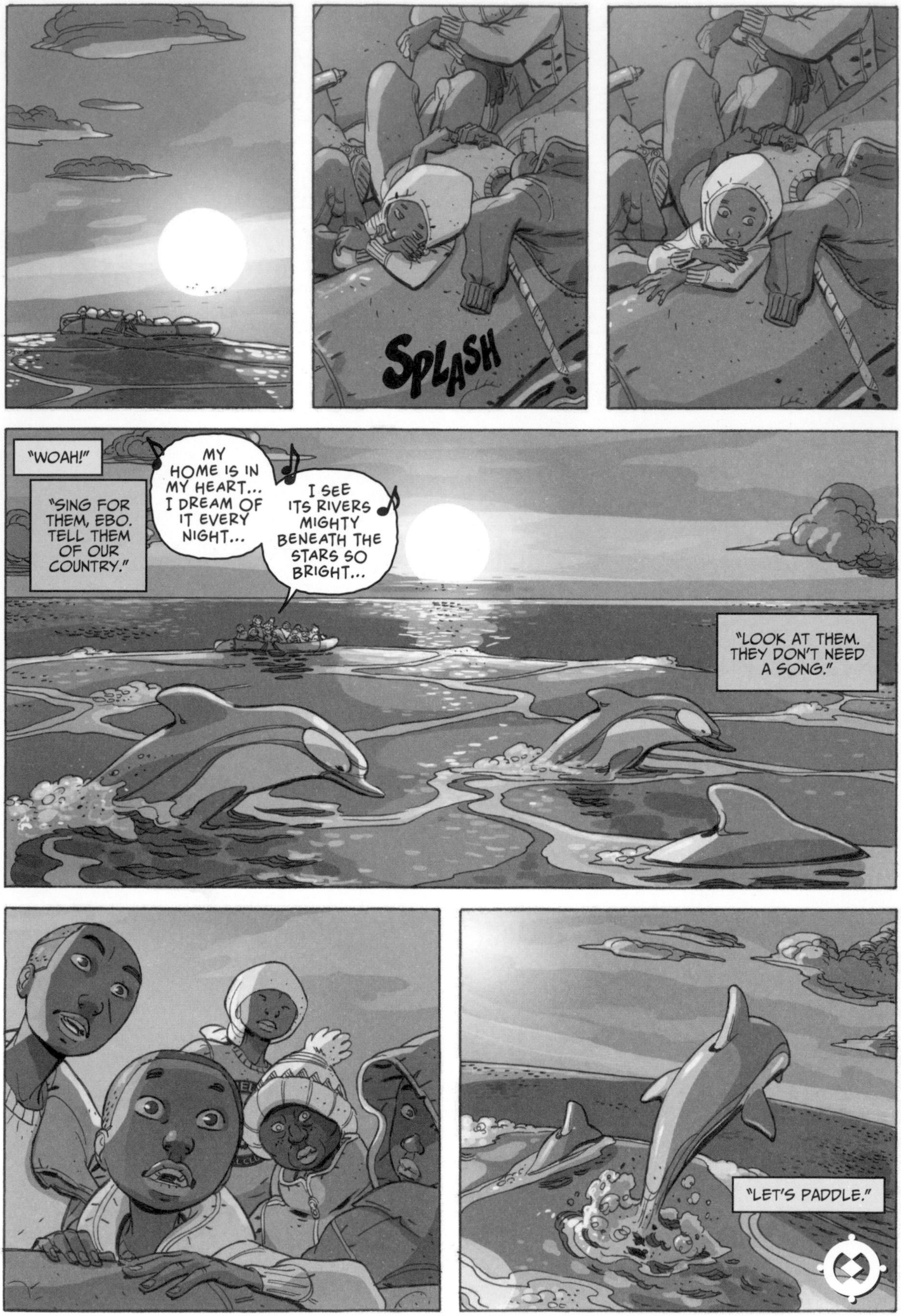
SPLASH
"WOAH!"
"SING FOR THEM, EBO. TELL THEM OF OUR COUNTRY."
MY HOME IS IN MY HEART... I DREAM OF IT EVERY NIGHT...
I SEE ITS RIVERS MIGHTY BENEATH THE STARS SO BRIGHT...
"LOOK AT THEM. THEY DON'T NEED A SONG."
"LET'S PADDLE."

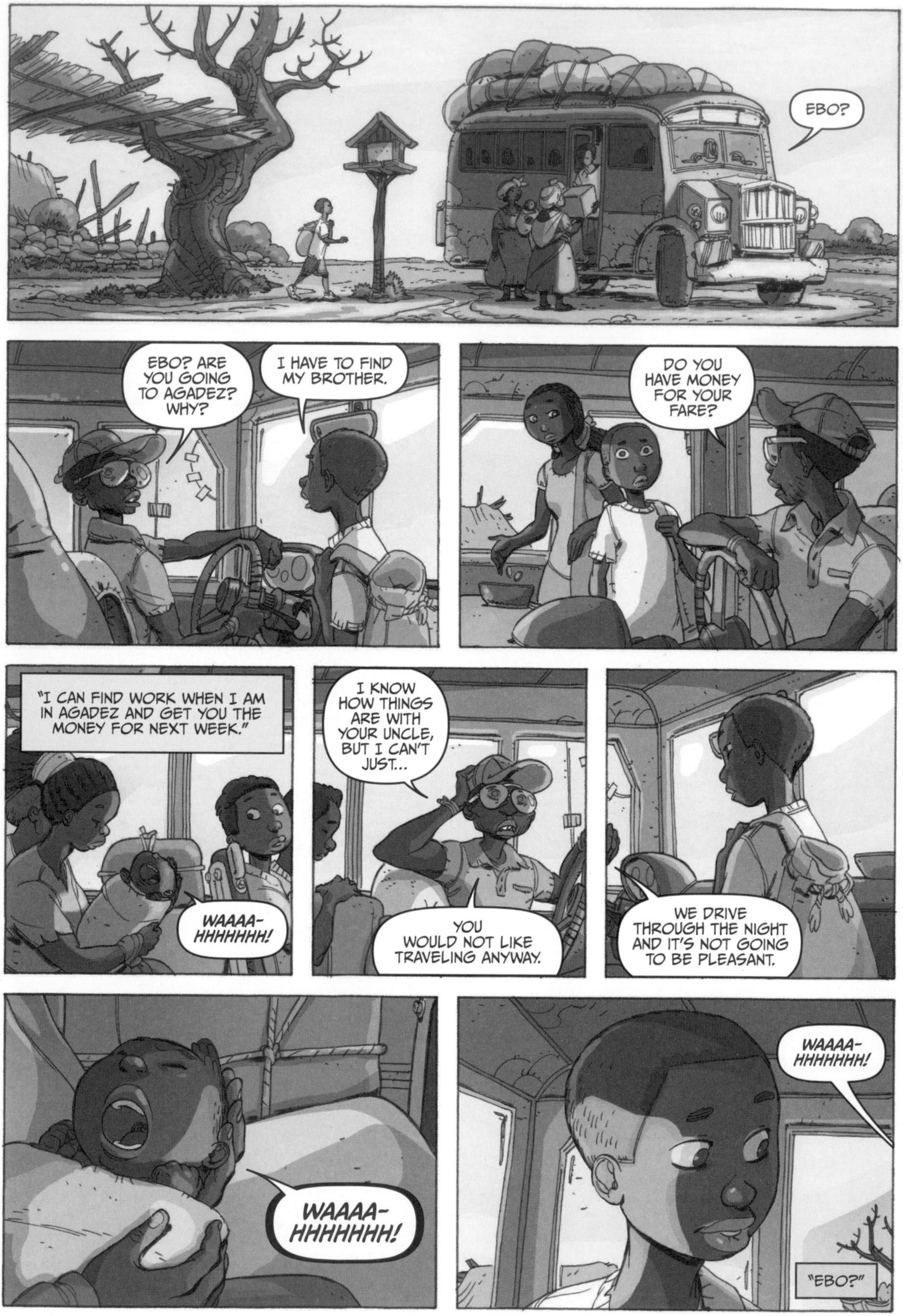
EBO?
EBO? ARE YOU GOING TO AGADEZ? WHY?
I HAVE TO FIND MY BROTHER.
DO YOU HAVE MONEY FOR YOUR FARE?
"I CAN FIND WORK WHEN I AM IN AGADEZ AND GET YOU THE MONEY FOR NEXT WEEK."
WAAAA-HHHHHHH!
I KNOW HOW THINGS ARE WITH YOUR UNCLE, BUT I CAN'T JUST...
YOU WOULD NOT LIKE TRAVELING ANYWAY.
WE DRIVE THROUGH THE NIGHT AND IT'S NOT GOING TO BE PLEASANT.
WAAAA-HHHHHHH!
WAAAA-HHHHHHH!
"EBO?"

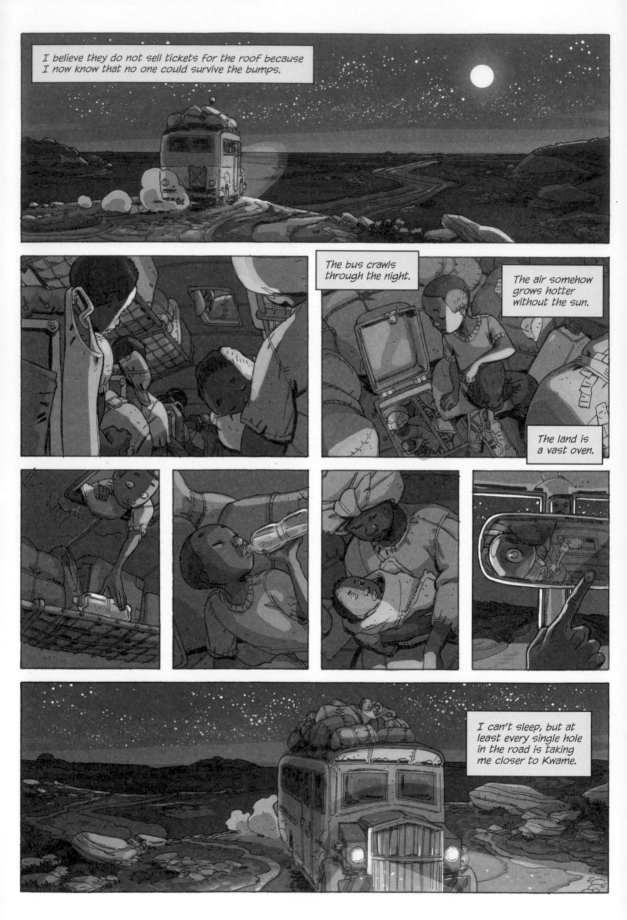

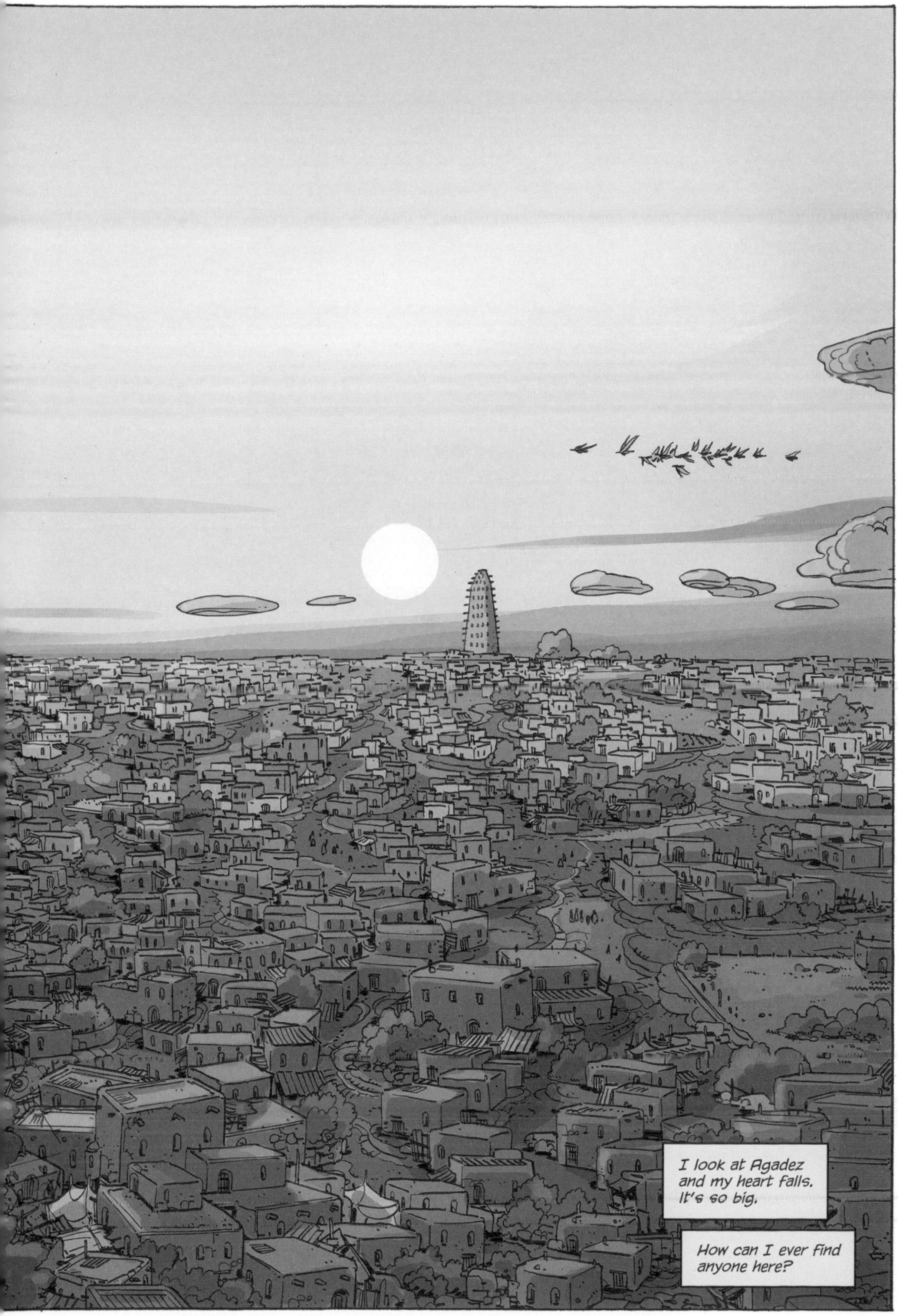
I look at Agadez and my heart falls. It's so big.
How can I ever find anyone here?

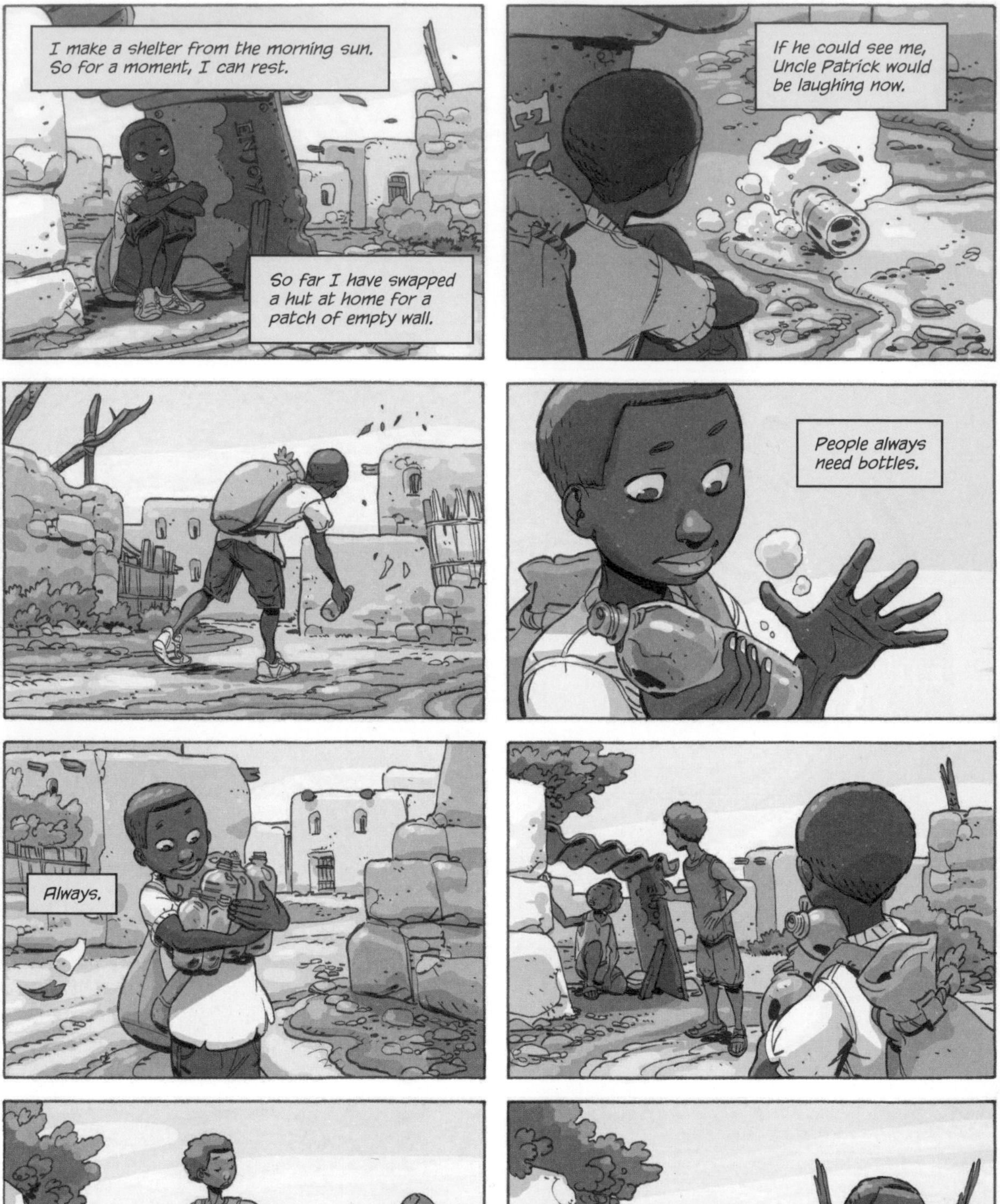
I make a shelter from the morning sun. So for a moment, I can rest.
So far I have swapped a hut at home for a patch of empty wall.
If he could see me, Uncle Patrick would be laughing now.
People always need bottles.
Always.

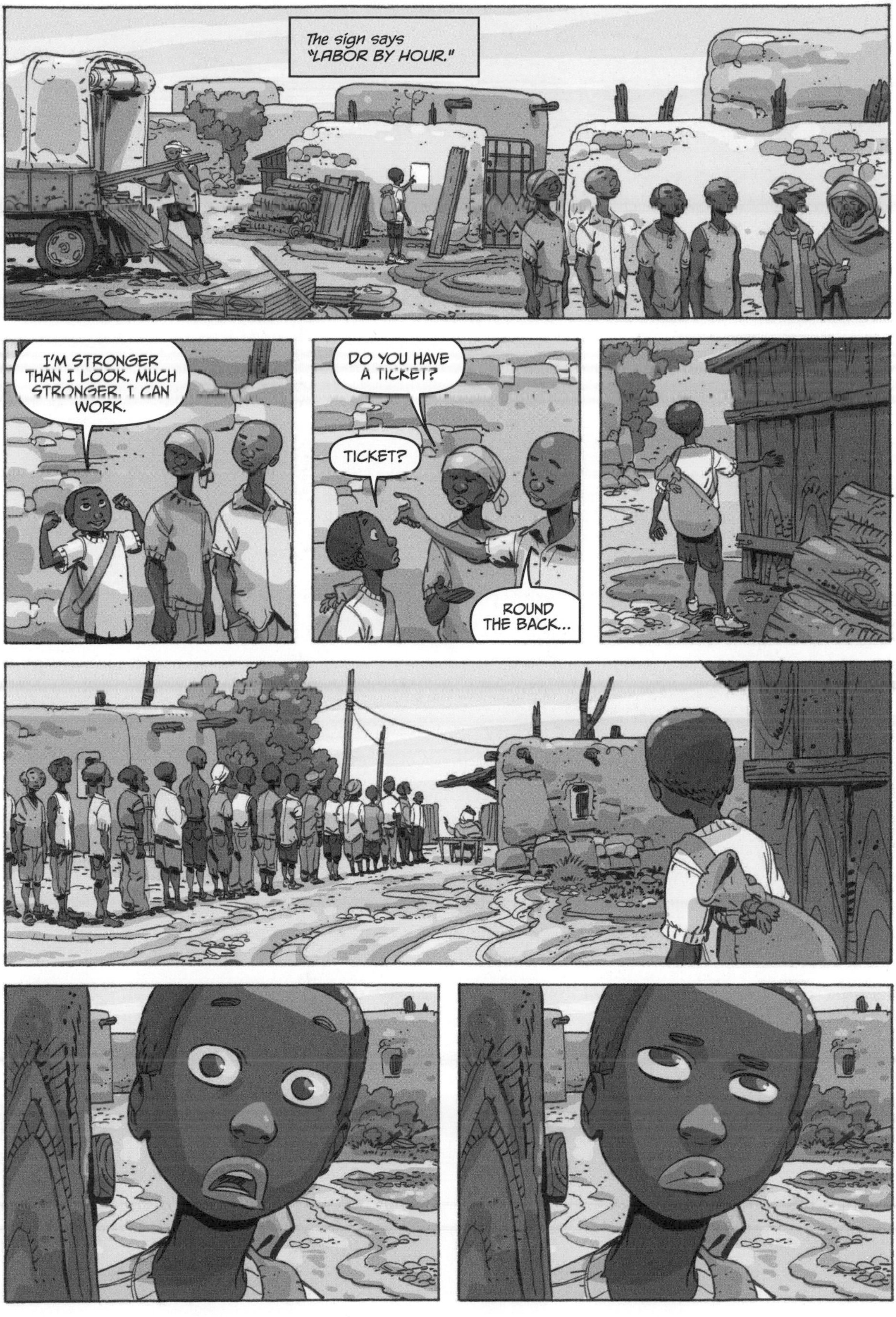
The sign says "LABOR BY HOUR."
I'M STRONGER THAN I LOOK. MUCH STRONGER. I CAN WORK.
DO YOU HAVE A TICKET?
TICKET?
ROUND THE BACK...

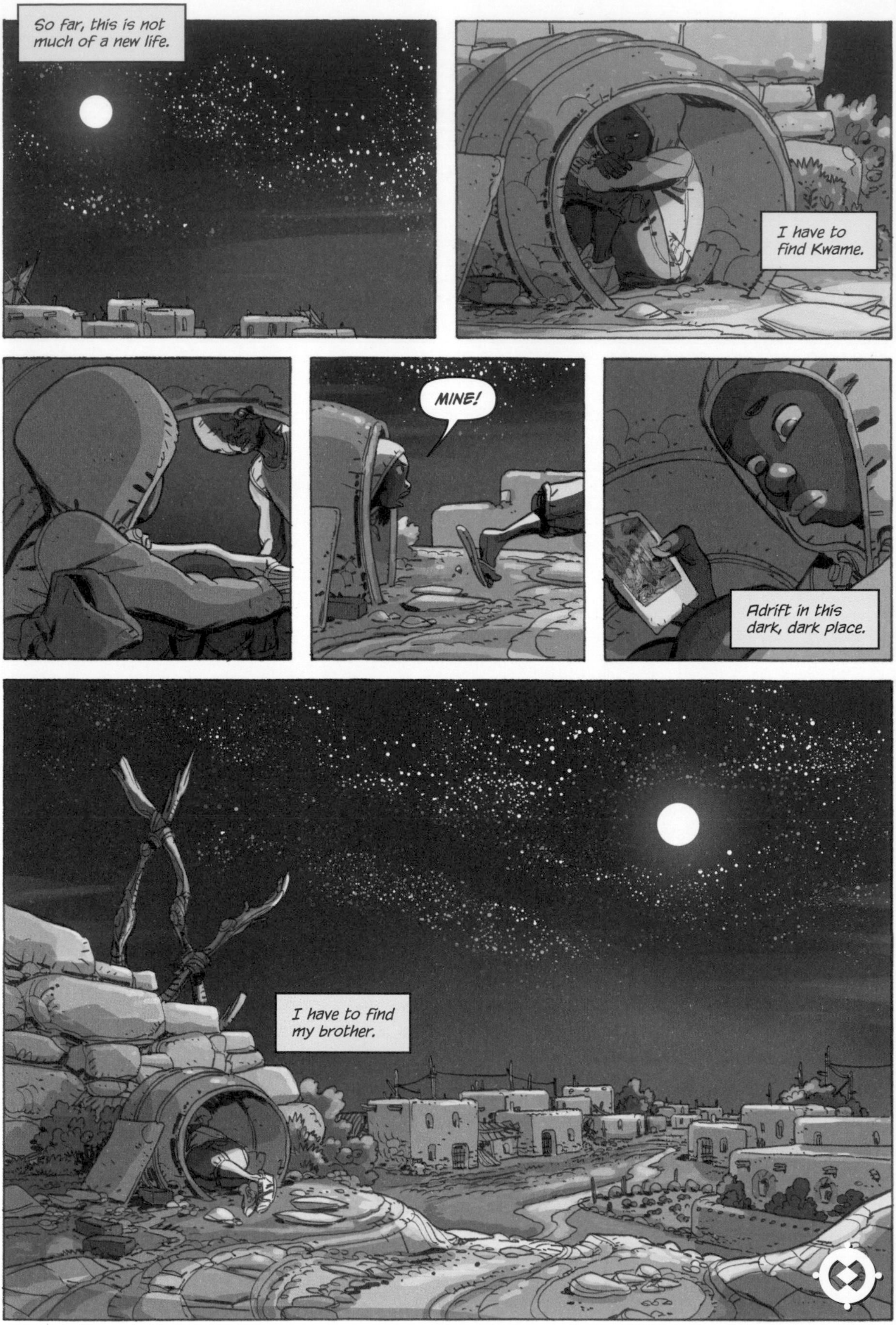
So far, this is not much of a new life.
I have to find Kwame.
MINE!
Adrift in this dark, dark place.
I have to find my brother.

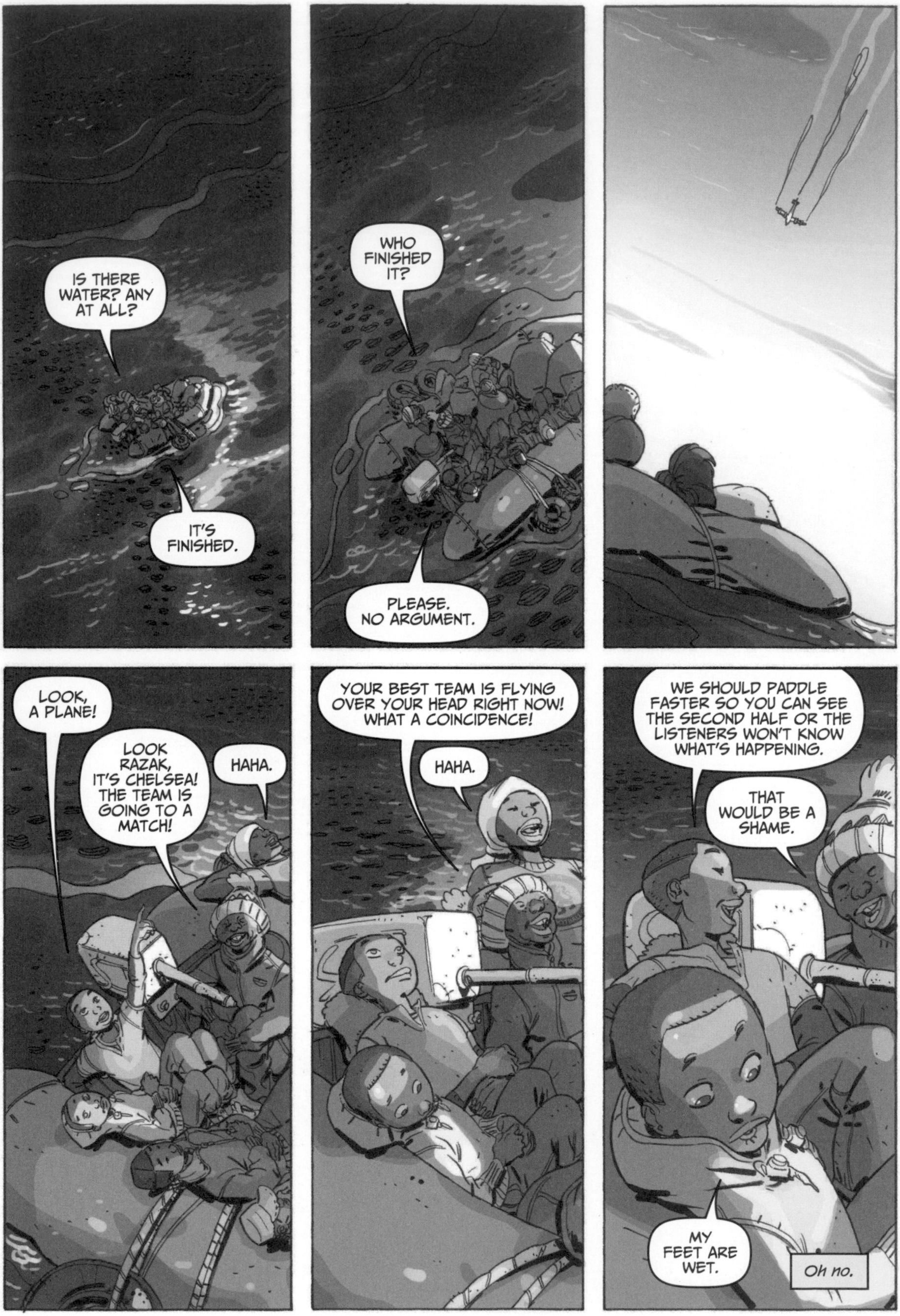
IS THERE WATER? ANY AT ALL?
IT'S FINISHED.
WHO FINISHED IT?
PLEASE. NO ARGUMENT.
LOOK, A PLANE!
LOOK RAZAK, IT'S CHELSEA! THE TEAM IS GOING TO A MATCH!
HAHA.
YOUR BEST TEAM IS FLYING OVER YOUR HEAD RIGHT NOW! WHAT A COINCIDENCE!
HAHA.
WE SHOULD PADDLE FASTER SO YOU CAN SEE THE SECOND HALF OR THE LISTENERS WON'T KNOW WHAT'S HAPPENING.
THAT WOULD BE A SHAME.
MY FEET ARE WET.
Oh no.

I gasp for life.

I HAVE YOU, EBO.

Somehow we have all survived.

THANK YOU, THANK YOU FOR SAVING ME.

I AM AFRAID YOU ARE NOT MUCH BETTER OFF.

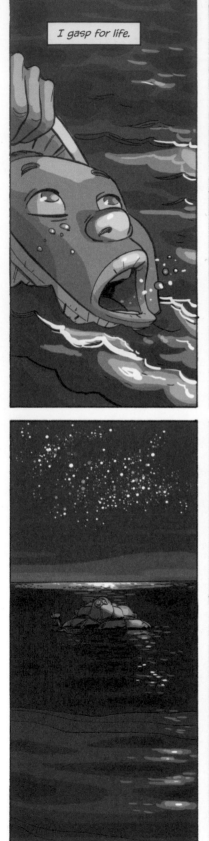

We have no food, water, or gas.

We are drifting on the tides, lost and alone.

WE'RE GOING TO DIE, AREN'T WE?

DON'T SAY IT, EBO. WE CAN'T GIVE UP, EVER. SISI WAITS FOR US.

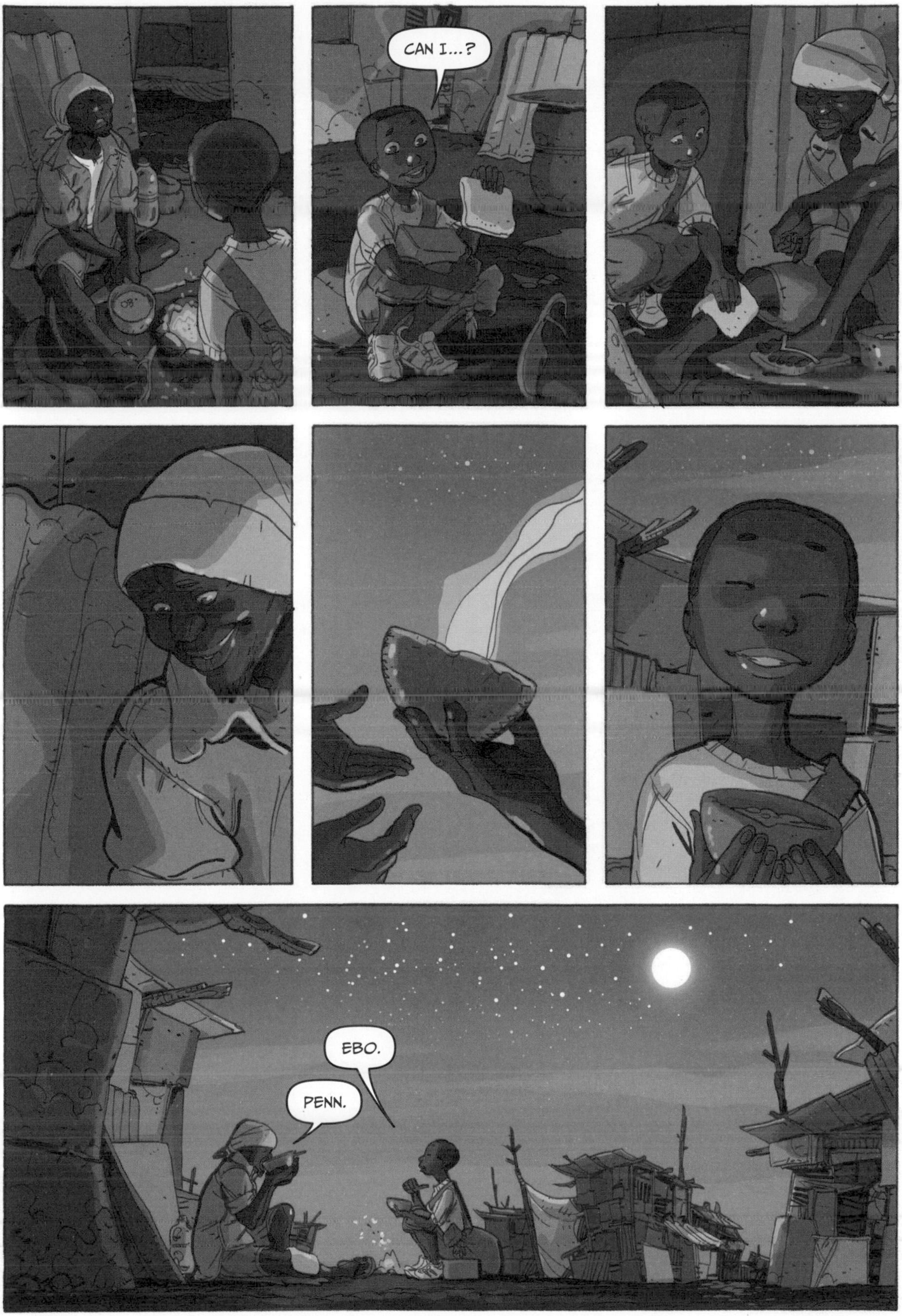
CAN I...?
EBO.
PENN.

38

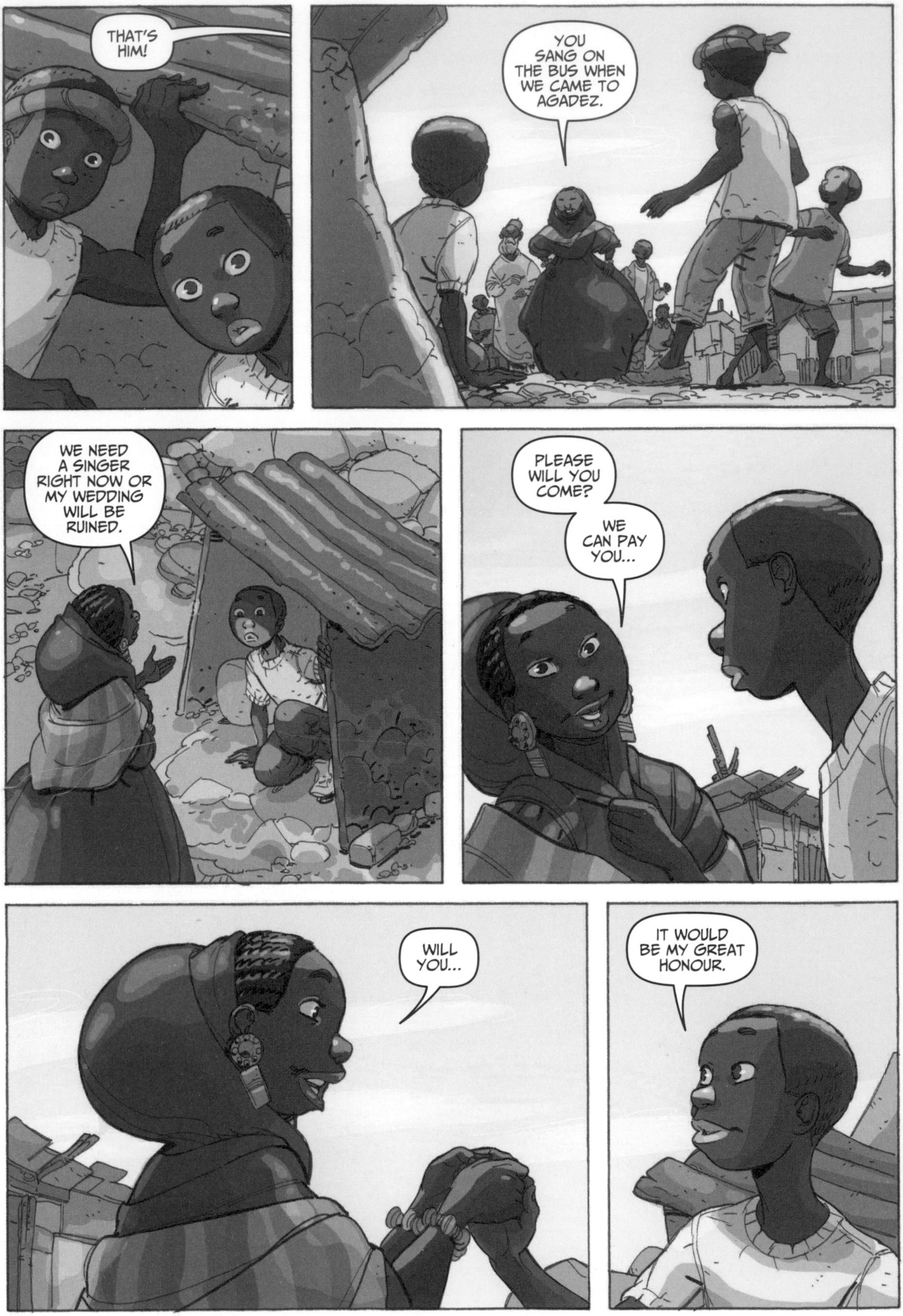
THAT'S HIM!
YOU SANG ON THE BUS WHEN WE CAME TO AGADEZ.
WE NEED A SINGER RIGHT NOW OR MY WEDDING WILL BE RUINED.
PLEASE WILL YOU COME?
WE CAN PAY YOU...
WILL YOU...
IT WOULD BE MY GREAT HONOUR.

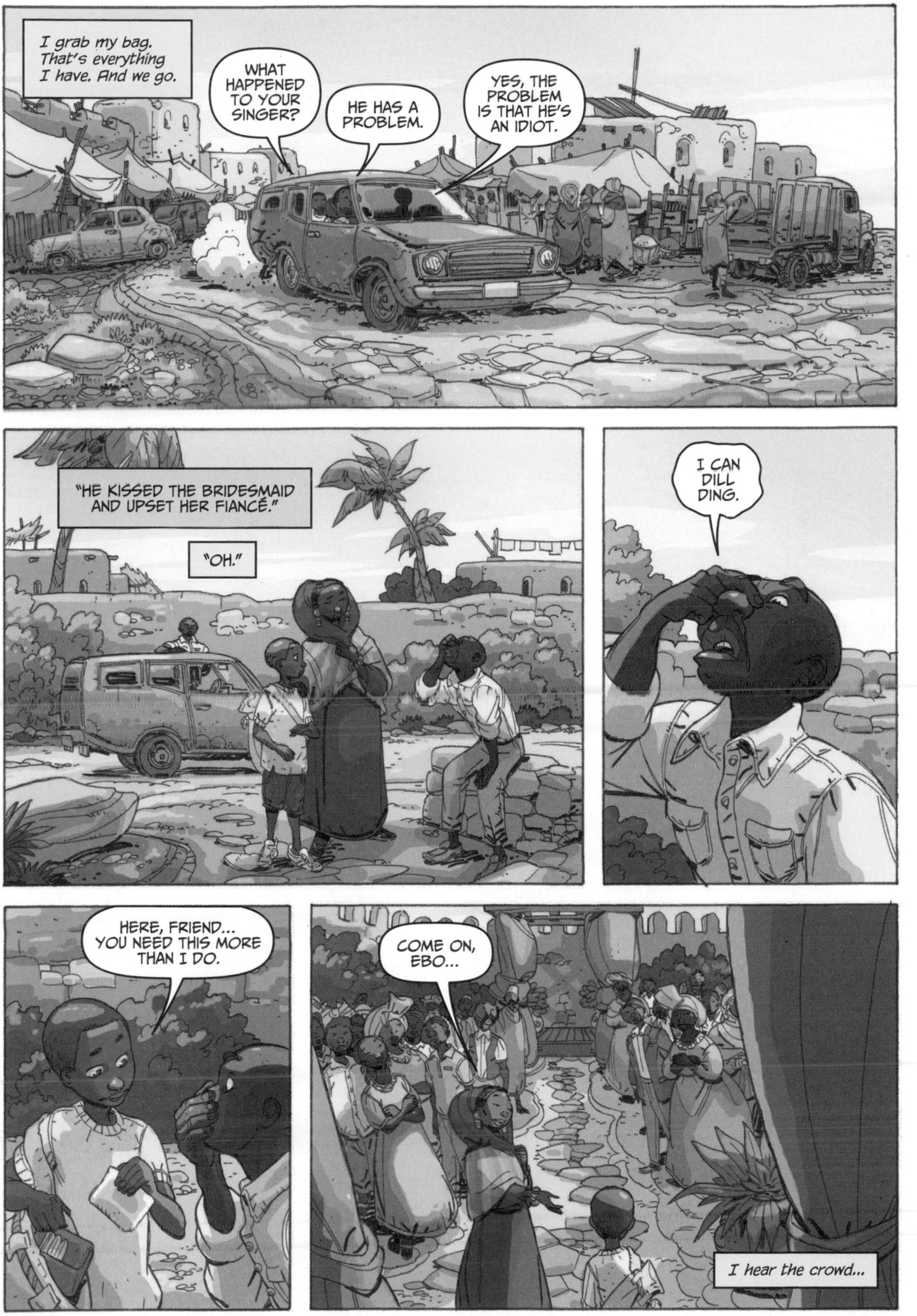
I grab my bag. That's everything I have. And we go.
WHAT HAPPENED TO YOUR SINGER?
HE HAS A PROBLEM.
YES, THE PROBLEM IS THAT HE'S AN IDIOT.
"HE KISSED THE BRIDESMAID AND UPSET HER FIANCÉ."
"OH."
I CAN DILL DING.
HERE, FRIEND... YOU NEED THIS MORE THAN I DO.
COME ON, EBO...
I hear the crowd...

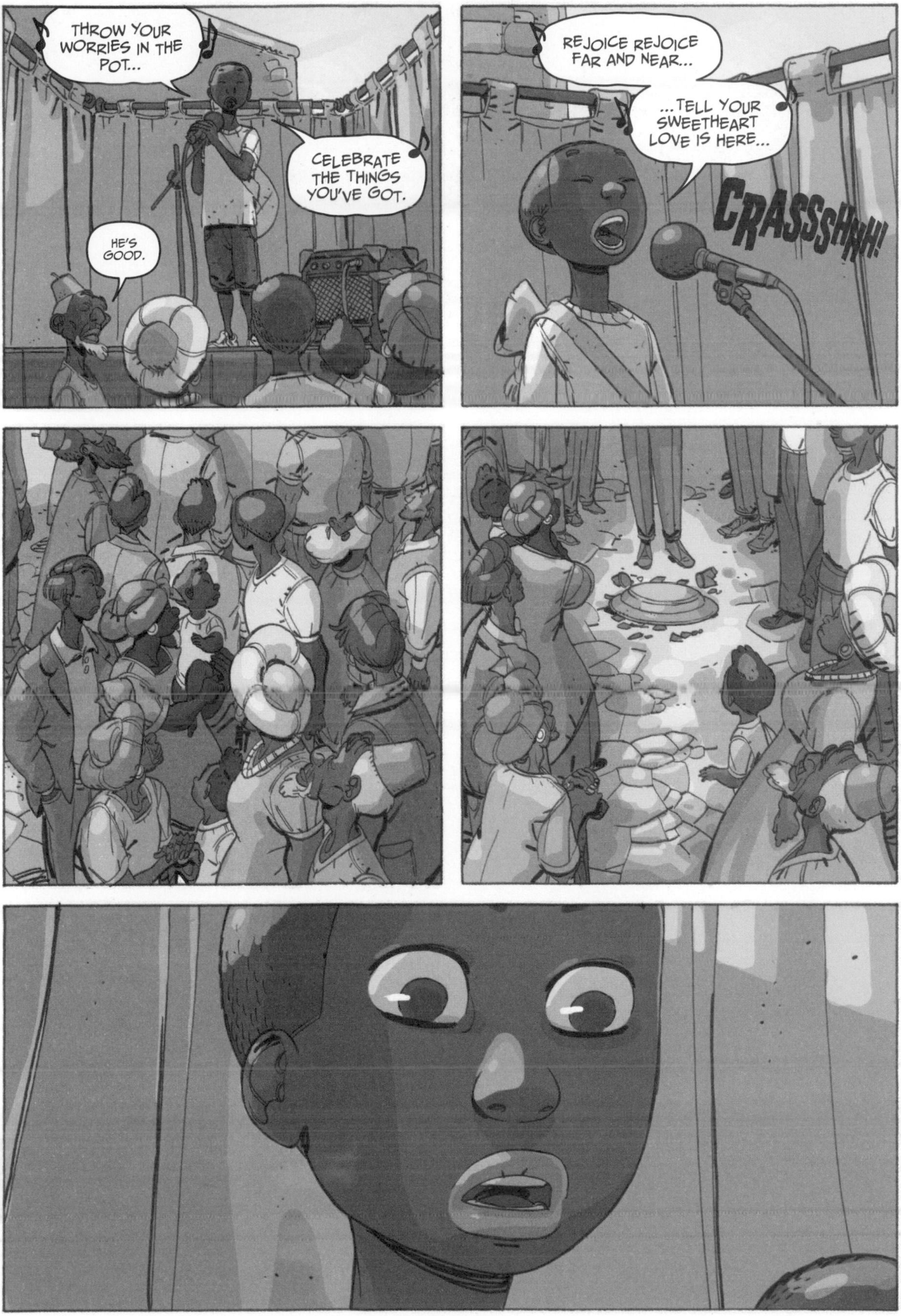
THROW YOUR WORRIES IN THE POT...
CELEBRATE THE THINGS YOU'VE GOT.
HE'S GOOD.
REJOICE REJOICE FAR AND NEAR...
...TELL YOUR SWEETHEART LOVE IS HERE...
CRASSSHHH!

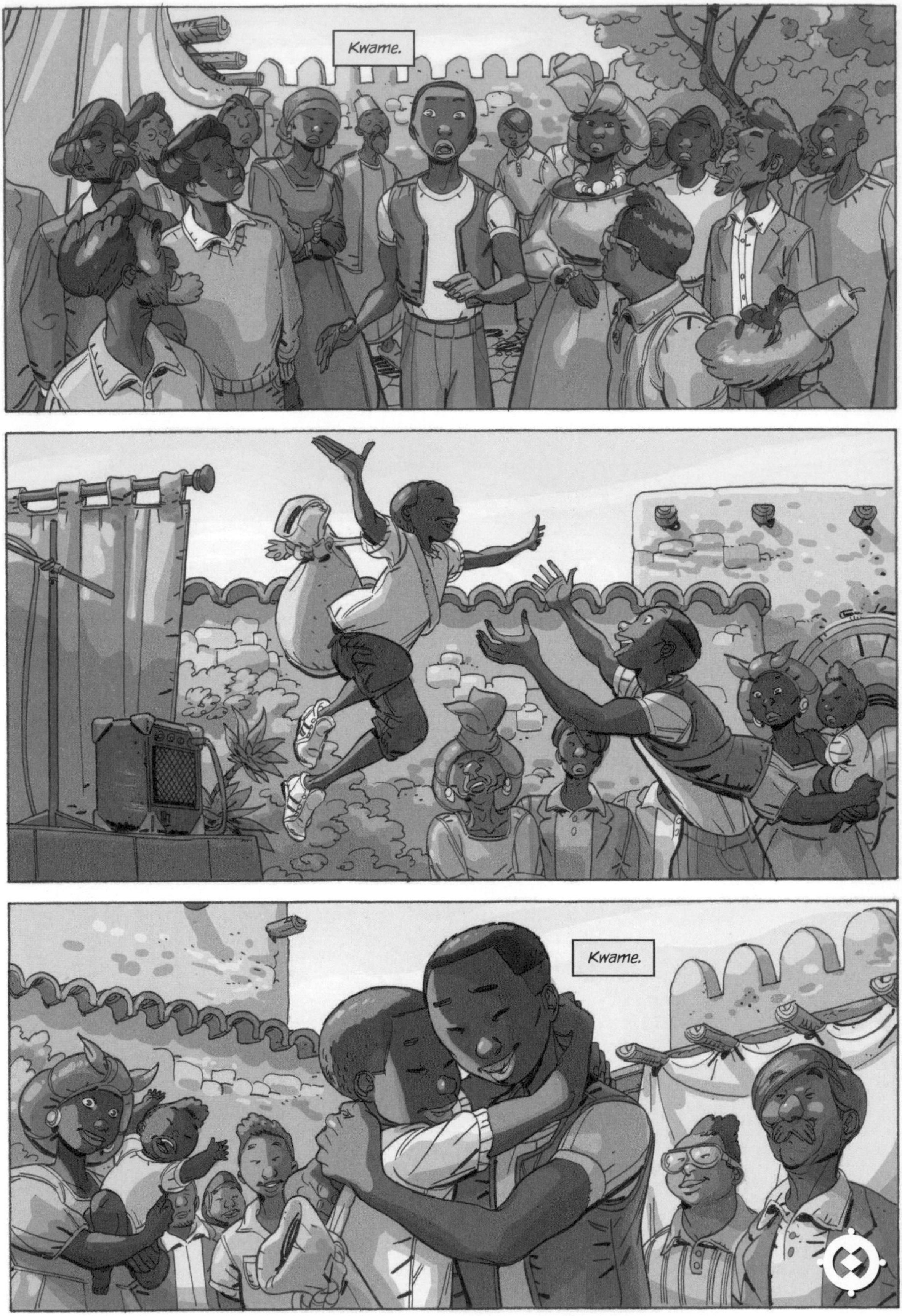
Kwame.
Kwame.

NOW

I hold on tight to Kwame.

CHAPTER 7

Around us, the night is pitch black.

I hold on to Kwame and I don't let go.

We drift in and out of banks of mist, clinging to the upside-down dinghy for our lives.

I'M F-F-F-FRREEZZZING.

Everyone is soaking wet and shivering with cold.

WE DON'T KNOW WHERE WE ARE, DO WE, EBO?

WE ARE ON OUR WAY, THAT'S WHERE WE ARE.

THINGS COULD BE WORSE FOR US.

WORSE? HOW COULD THINGS BE WORSE?

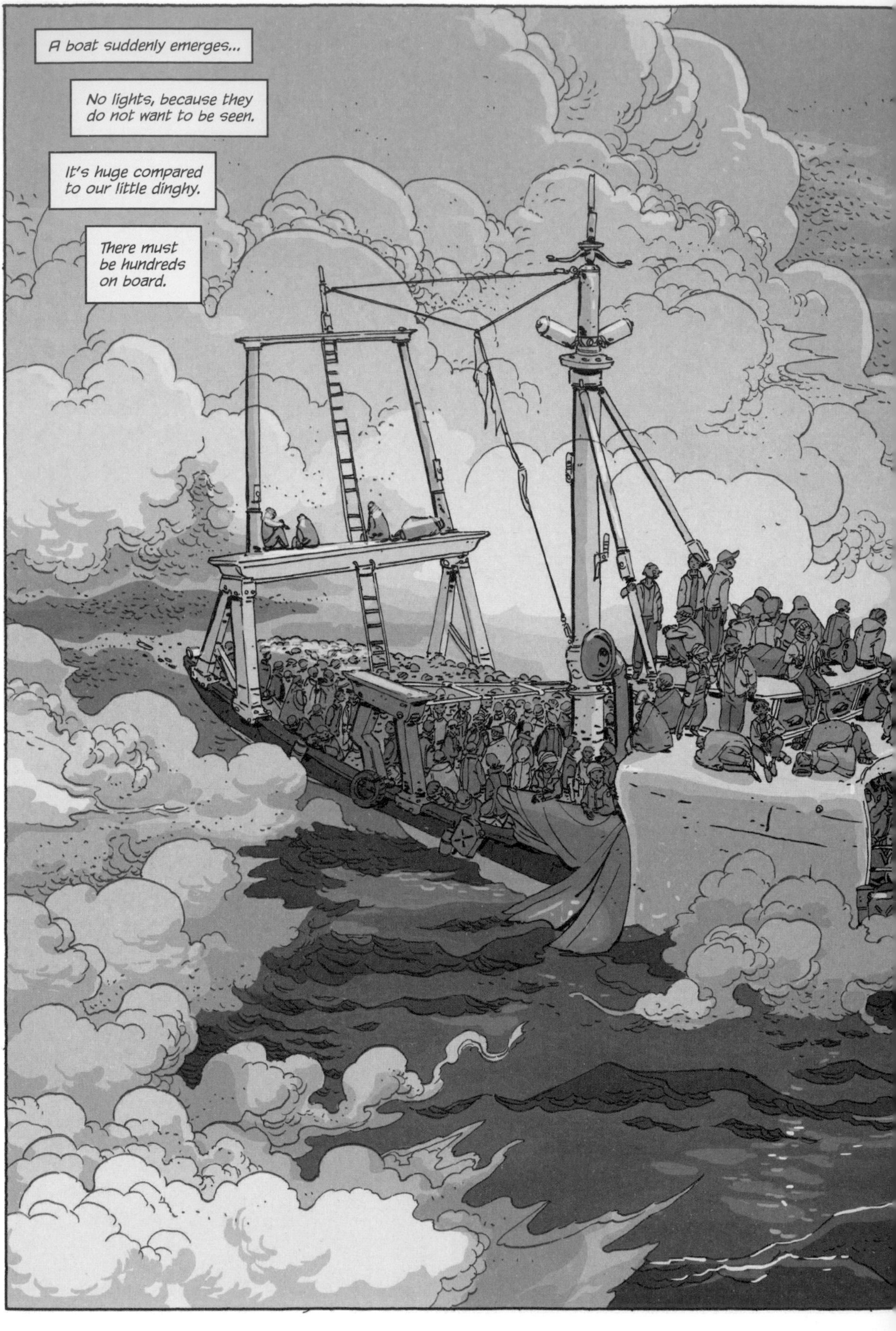
A boat suddenly emerges...
No lights, because they do not want to be seen.
It's huge compared to our little dinghy.
There must be hundreds on board.

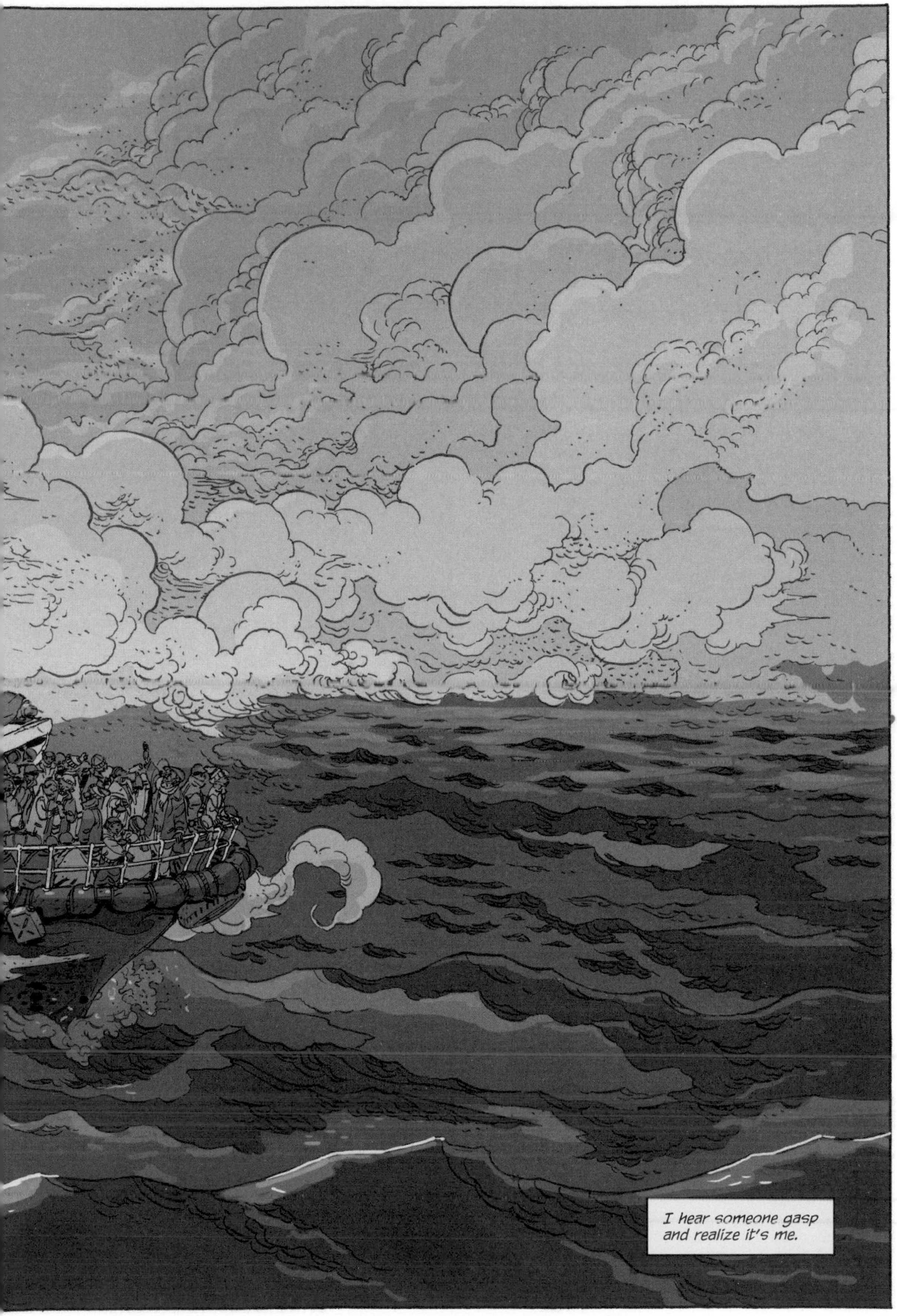
I hear someone gasp
and realize it's me.

52

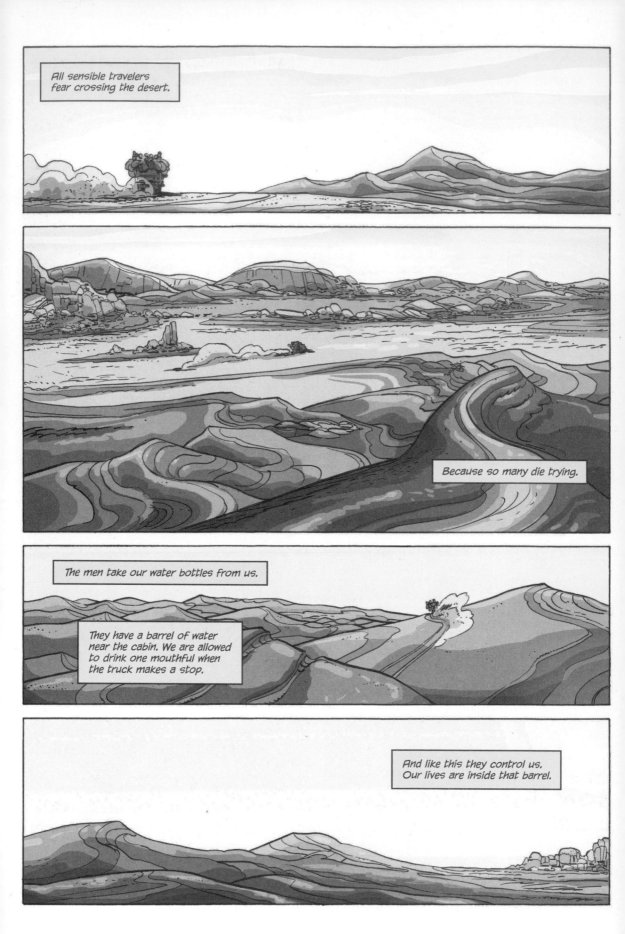

All sensible travelers fear crossing the desert.

Because so many die trying.

The men take our water bottles from us.

They have a barrel of water near the cabin. We are allowed to drink one mouthful when the truck makes a stop.

And like this they control us. Our lives are inside that barrel.

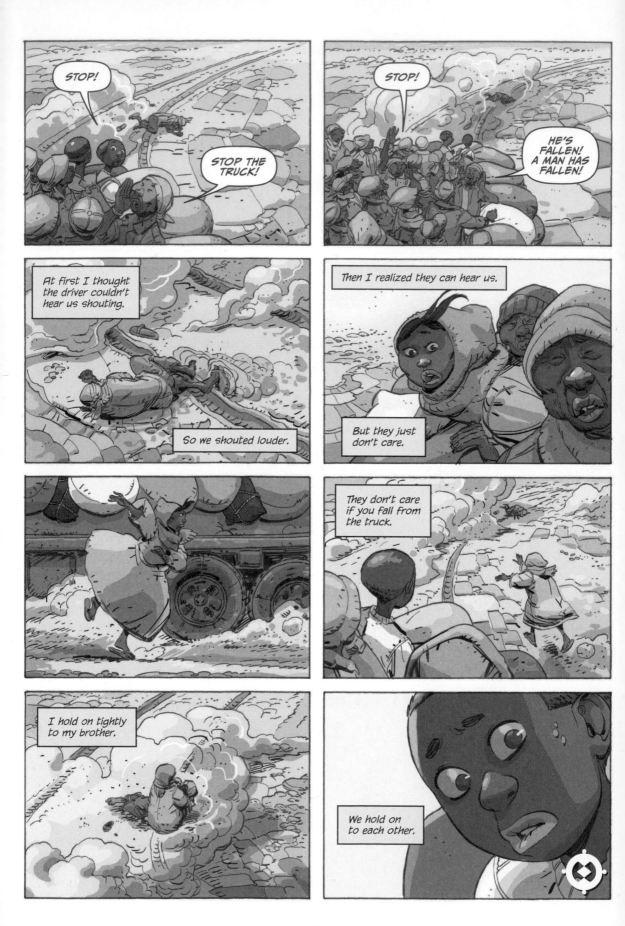

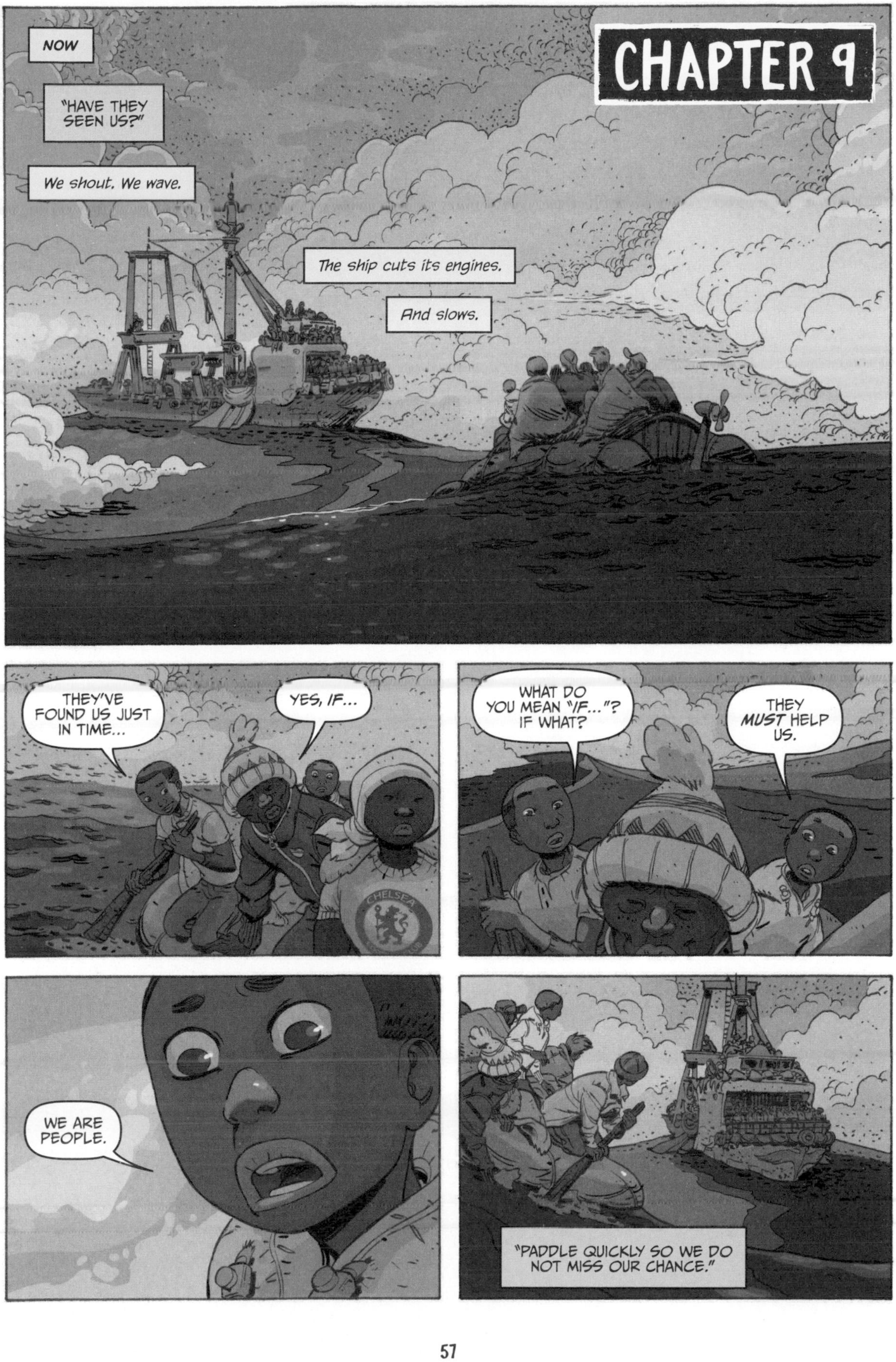
NOW
CHAPTER 9
"HAVE THEY SEEN US?"
We shout. We wave.
The ship cuts its engines.
And slows.
THEY'VE FOUND US JUST IN TIME...
YES, *IF*...
WHAT DO YOU MEAN "*IF*..."? IF WHAT?
THEY *MUST* HELP US.
WE ARE PEOPLE.
"PADDLE QUICKLY SO WE DO NOT MISS OUR CHANCE."

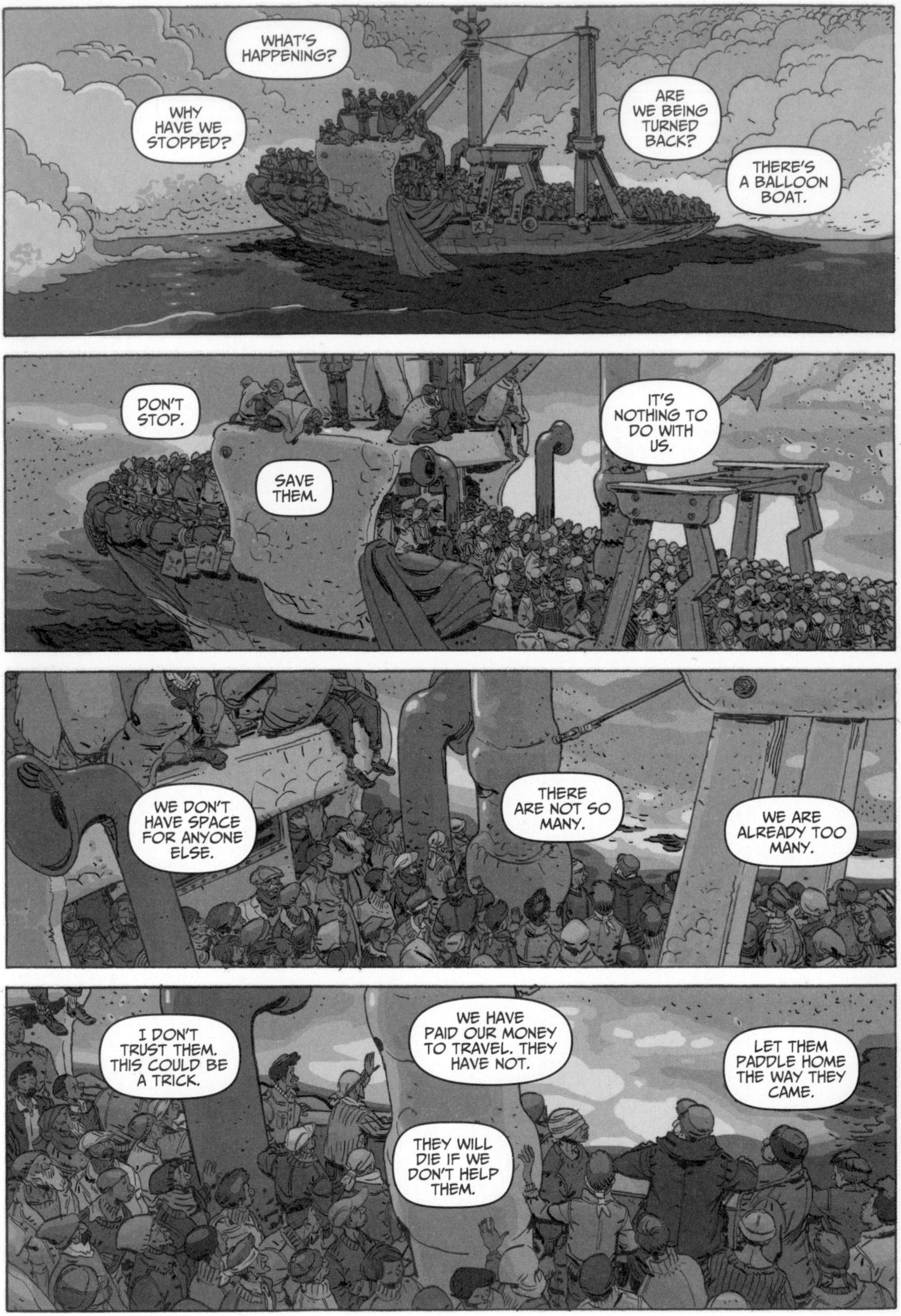
WHAT'S HAPPENING?
WHY HAVE WE STOPPED?
ARE WE BEING TURNED BACK?
THERE'S A BALLOON BOAT.
DON'T STOP.
SAVE THEM.
IT'S NOTHING TO DO WITH US.
WE DON'T HAVE SPACE FOR ANYONE ELSE.
THERE ARE NOT SO MANY.
WE ARE ALREADY TOO MANY.
I DON'T TRUST THEM. THIS COULD BE A TRICK.
WE HAVE PAID OUR MONEY TO TRAVEL. THEY HAVE NOT.
THEY WILL DIE IF WE DON'T HELP THEM.
LET THEM PADDLE HOME THE WAY THEY CAME.

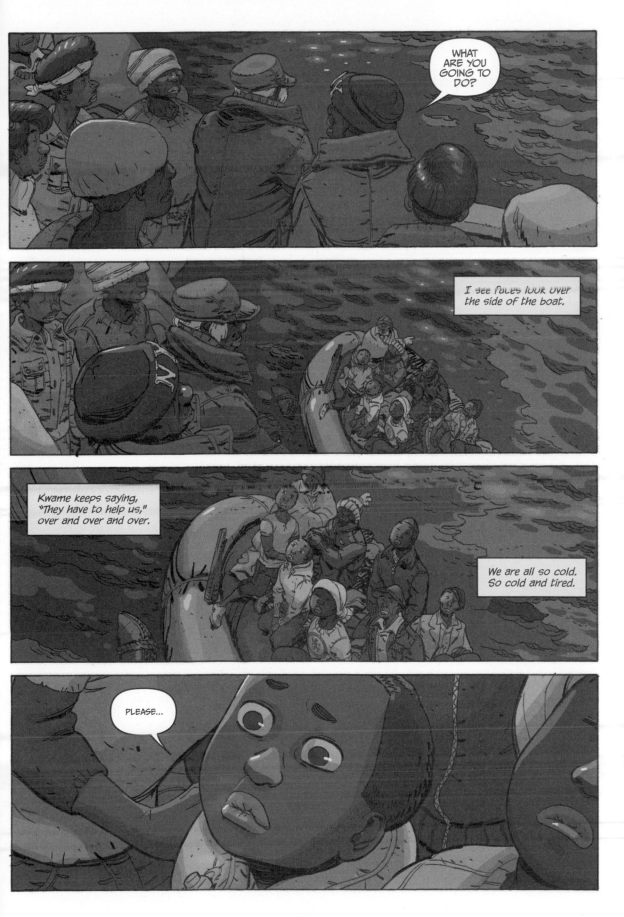

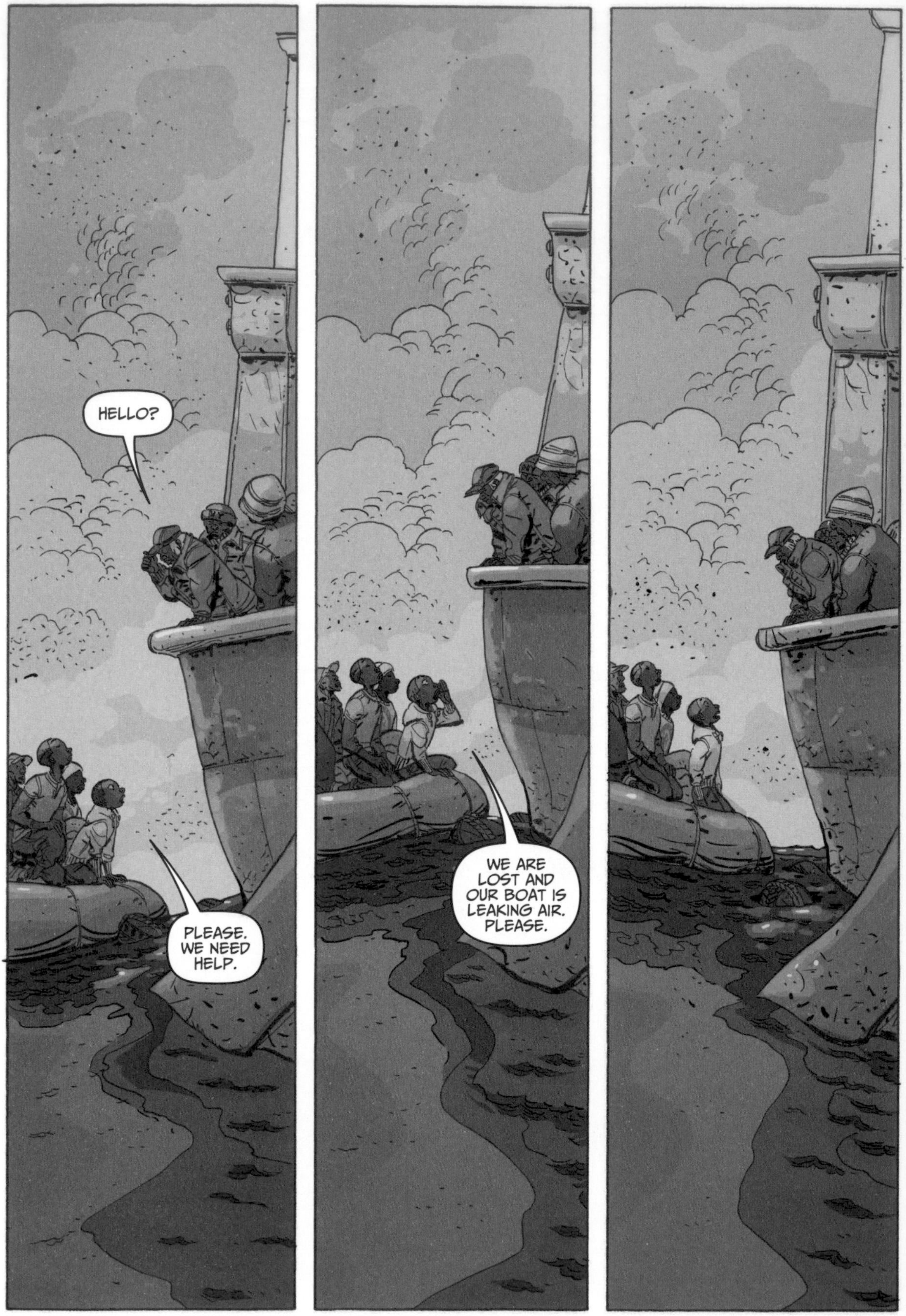
HELLO?
PLEASE. WE NEED HELP.
WE ARE LOST AND OUR BOAT IS LEAKING AIR. PLEASE.

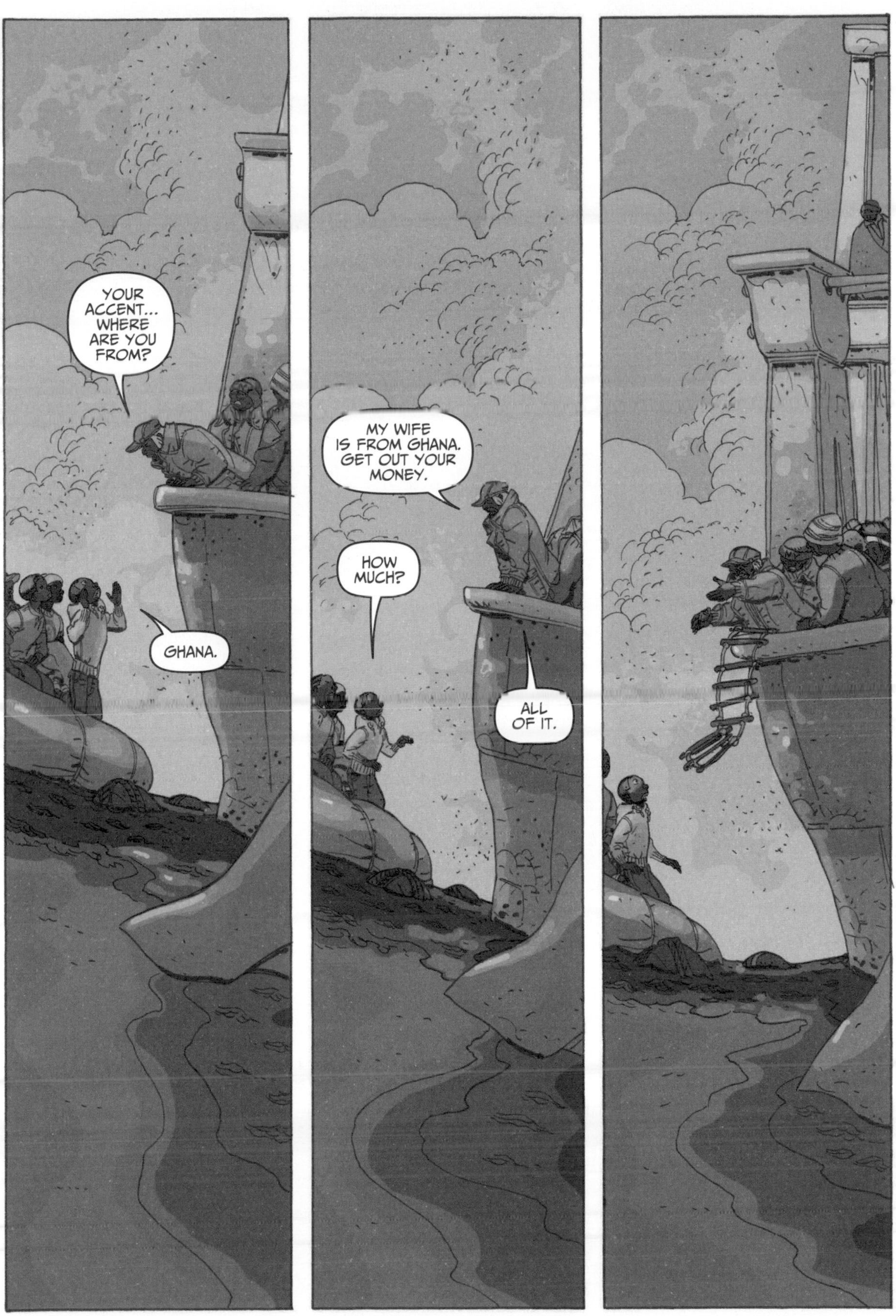
YOUR ACCENT... WHERE ARE YOU FROM?
GHANA.
MY WIFE IS FROM GHANA. GET OUT YOUR MONEY.
HOW MUCH?
ALL OF IT.

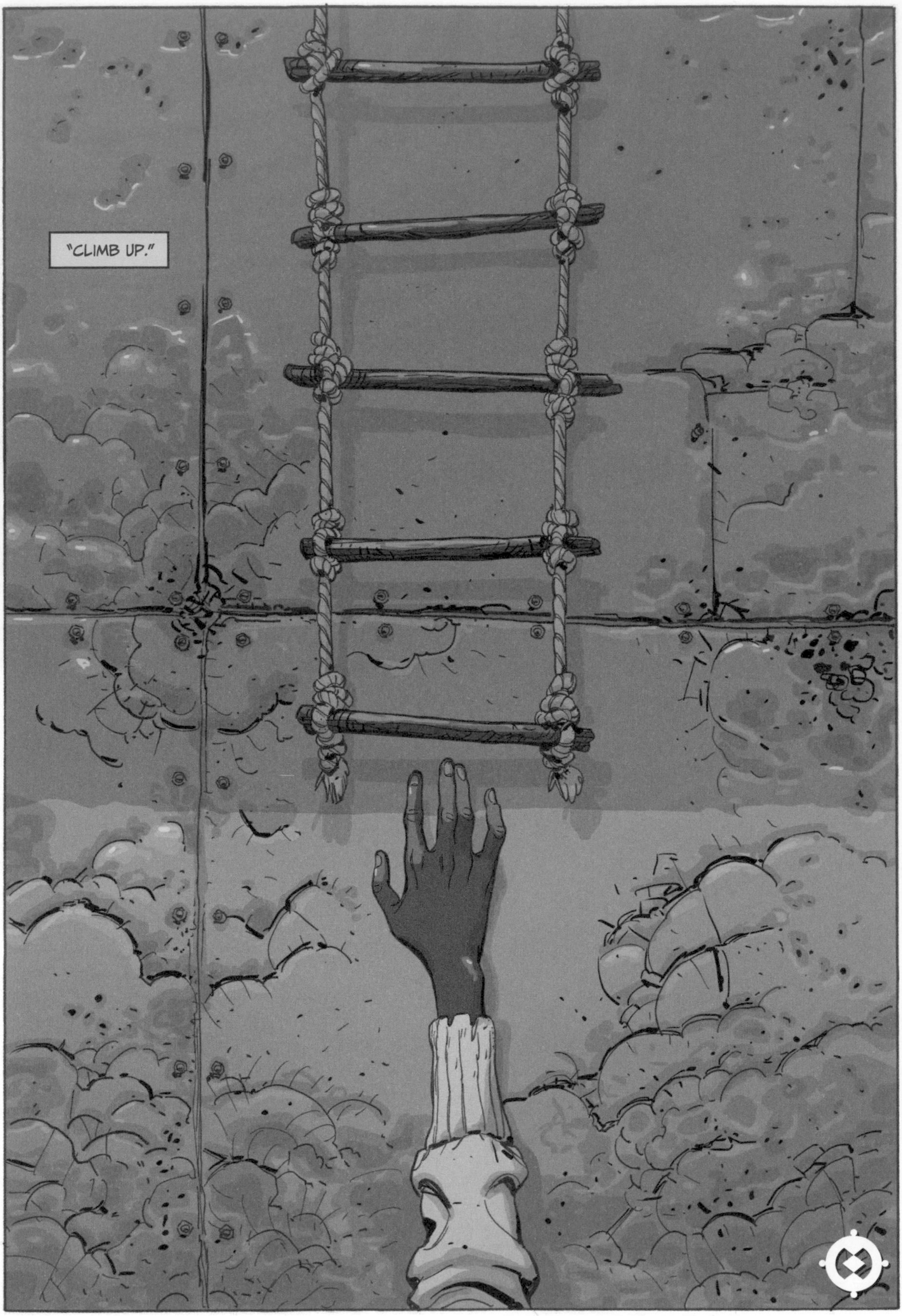
"CLIMB UP."

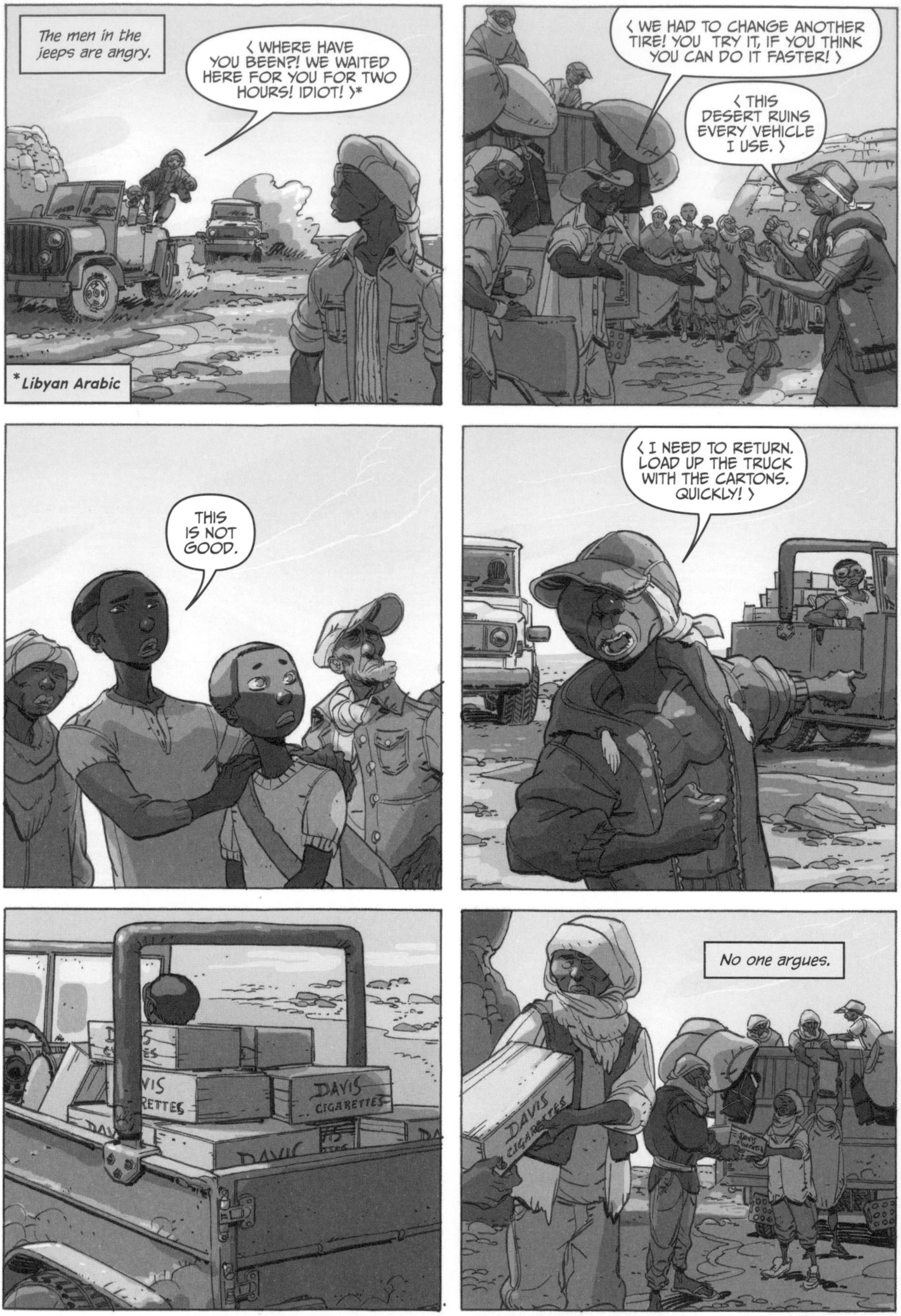

The men in the jeeps are angry.
‹ WHERE HAVE YOU BEEN?! WE WAITED HERE FOR YOU FOR TWO HOURS! IDIOT! ›*
*Libyan Arabic
‹ WE HAD TO CHANGE ANOTHER TIRE! YOU TRY IT, IF YOU THINK YOU CAN DO IT FASTER! ›
‹ THIS DESERT RUINS EVERY VEHICLE I USE. ›
THIS IS NOT GOOD.
‹ I NEED TO RETURN. LOAD UP THE TRUCK WITH THE CARTONS. QUICKLY! ›
DAVIS CIGARETTES
No one argues.
DAVIS CIGARETTES

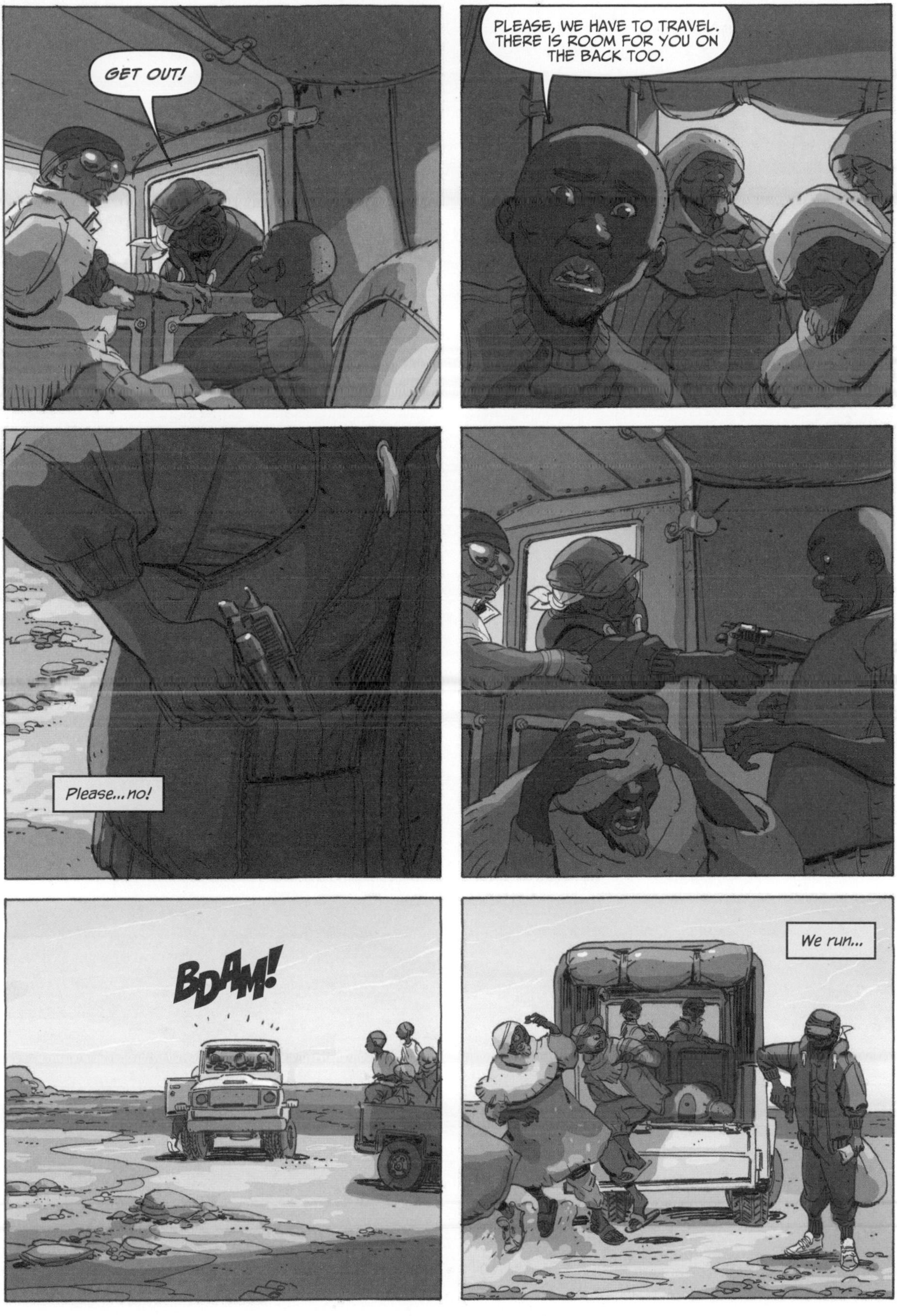
GET OUT!
PLEASE, WE HAVE TO TRAVEL. THERE IS ROOM FOR YOU ON THE BACK TOO.
Please...no!
BDAM!
We run...

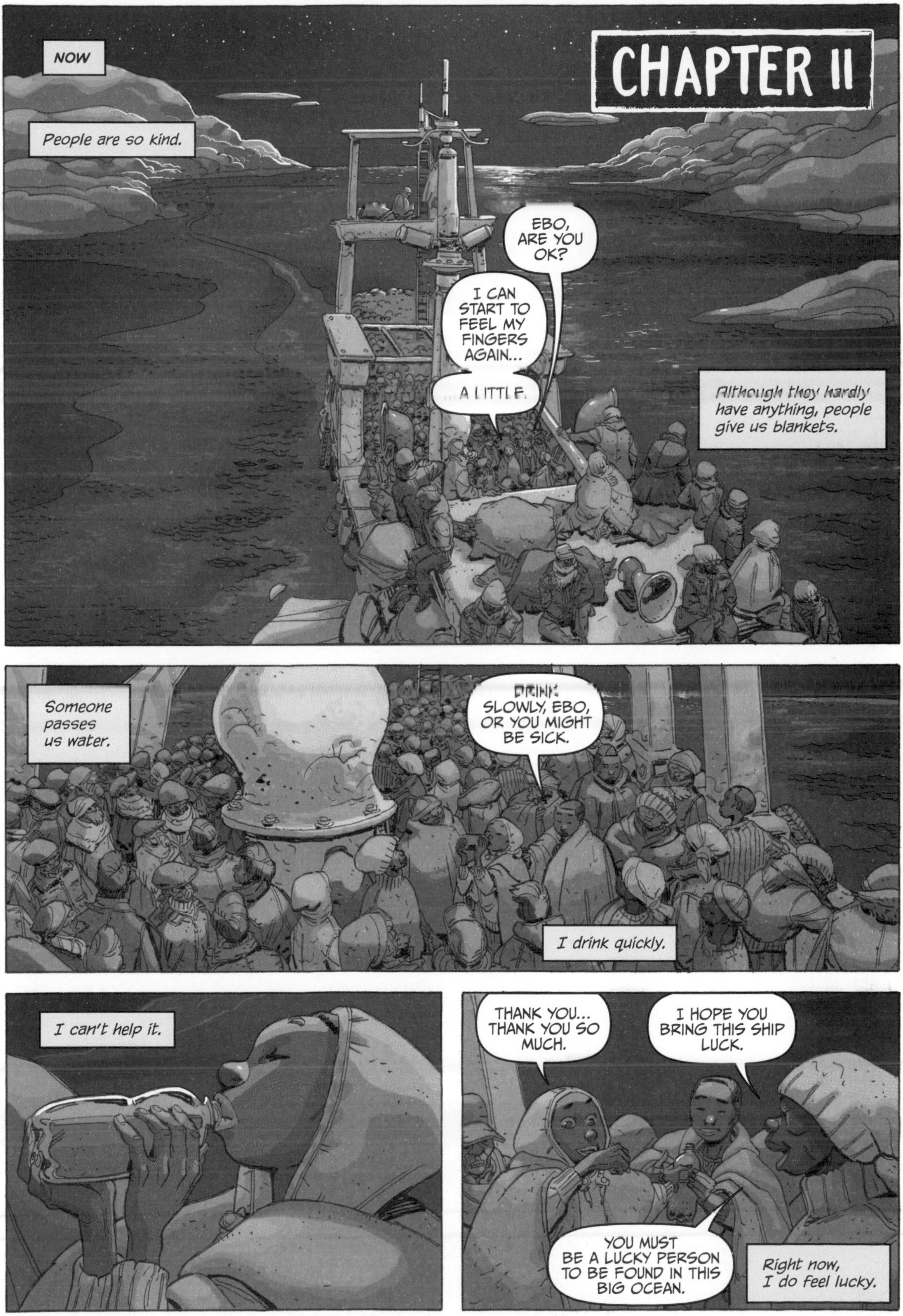
NOW
CHAPTER II
People are so kind.
EBO, ARE YOU OK?
I CAN START TO FEEL MY FINGERS AGAIN...
...A LITTLE.
Although they hardly have anything, people give us blankets.
Someone passes us water.
DRINK SLOWLY, EBO, OR YOU MIGHT BE SICK.
I drink quickly.
I can't help it.
THANK YOU... THANK YOU SO MUCH.
I HOPE YOU BRING THIS SHIP LUCK.
YOU MUST BE A LUCKY PERSON TO BE FOUND IN THIS BIG OCEAN.
Right now, I do feel lucky.

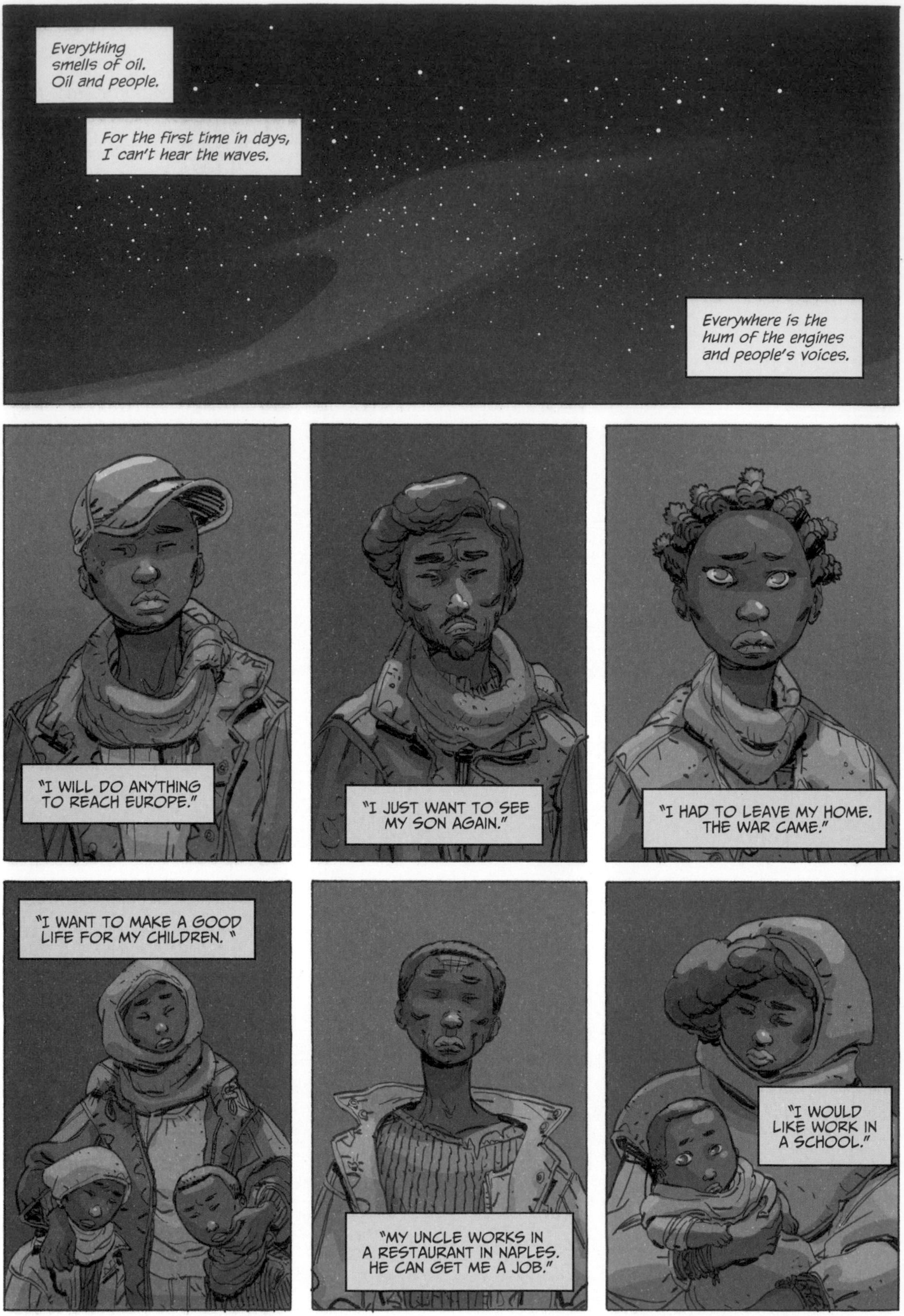

Everything smells of oil. Oil and people.
For the first time in days, I can't hear the waves.
Everywhere is the hum of the engines and people's voices.
"I WILL DO ANYTHING TO REACH EUROPE."
"I JUST WANT TO SEE MY SON AGAIN."
"I HAD TO LEAVE MY HOME. THE WAR CAME."
"I WANT TO MAKE A GOOD LIFE FOR MY CHILDREN. "
"MY UNCLE WORKS IN A RESTAURANT IN NAPLES. HE CAN GET ME A JOB."
"I WOULD LIKE WORK IN A SCHOOL."

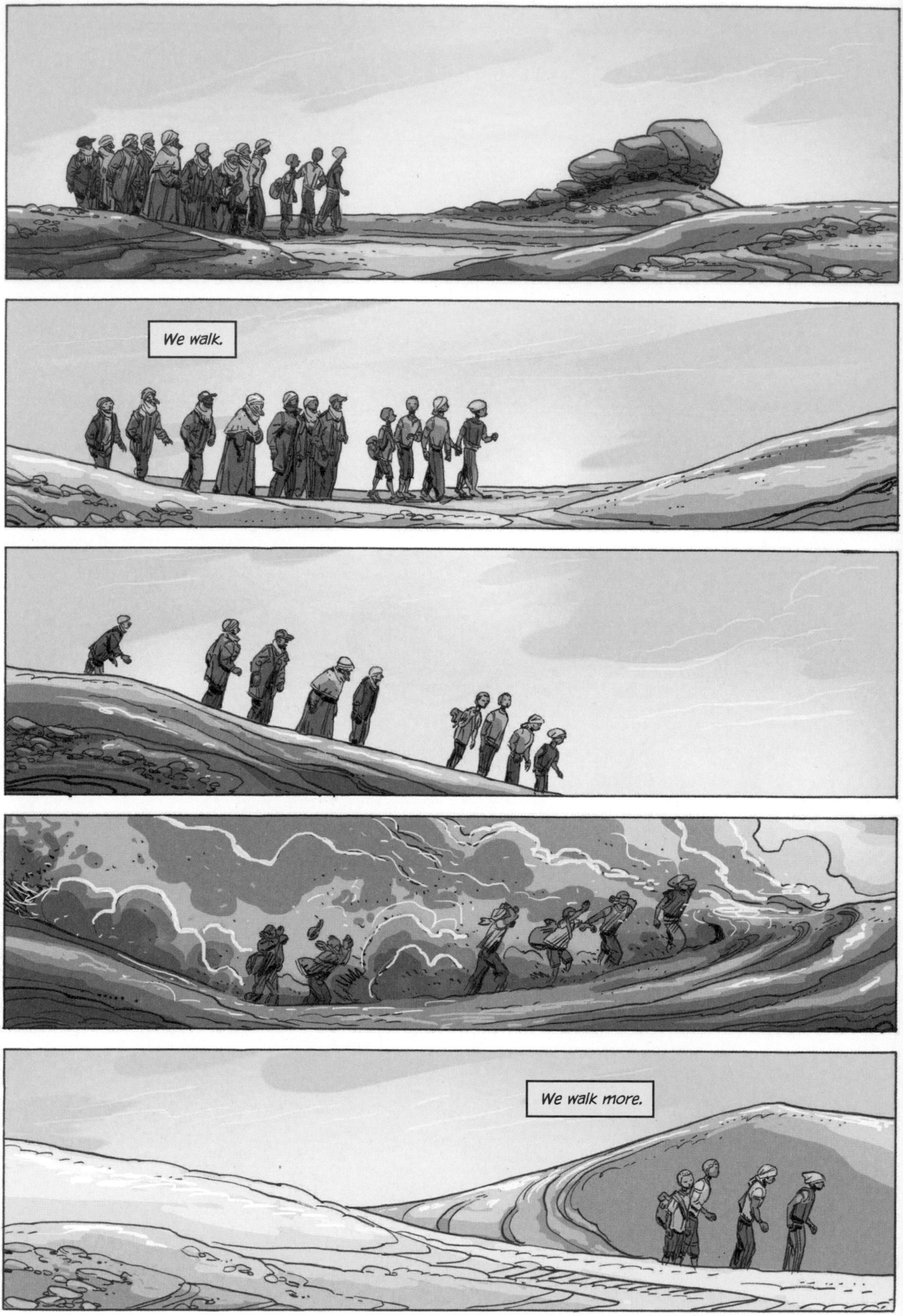
We walk.
We walk more.

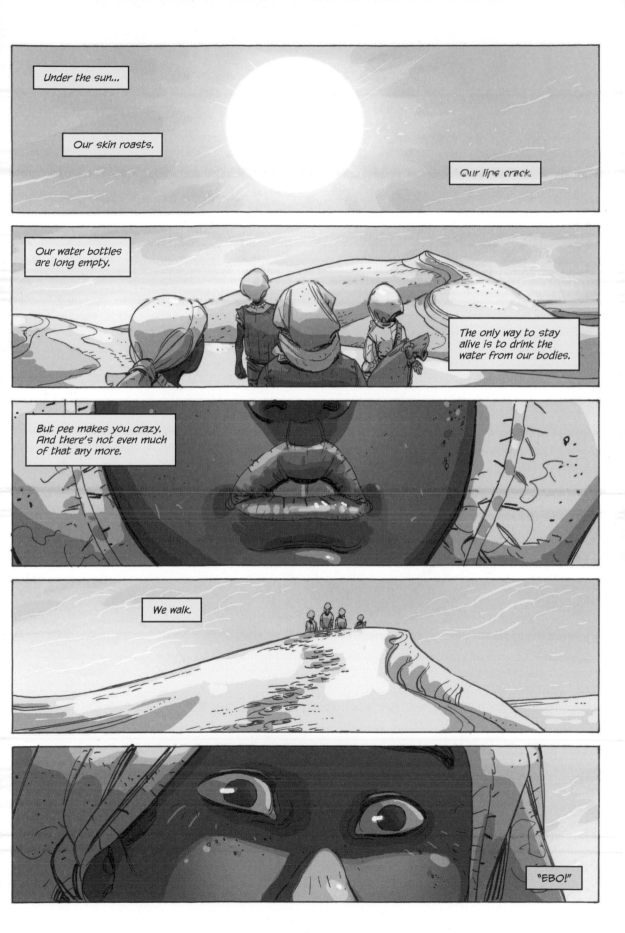

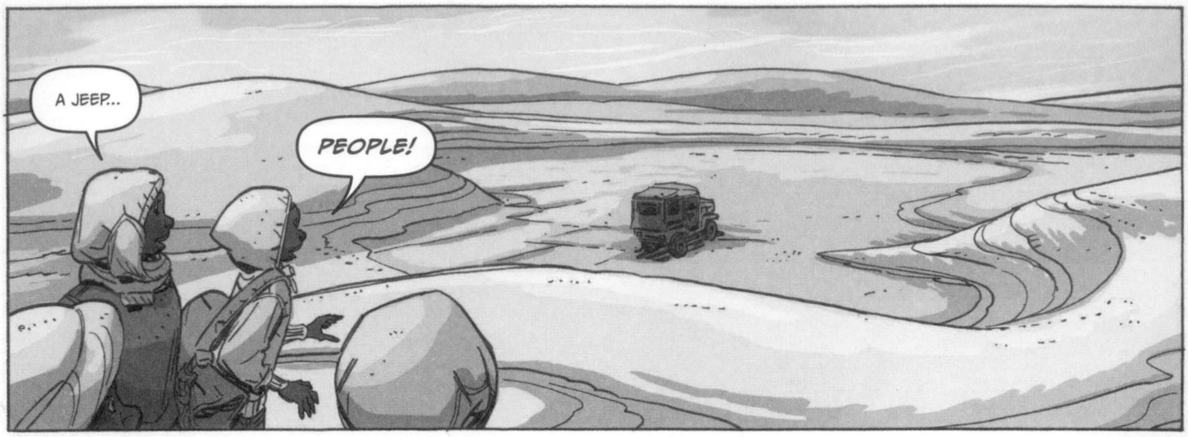
A JEEP...
PEOPLE!

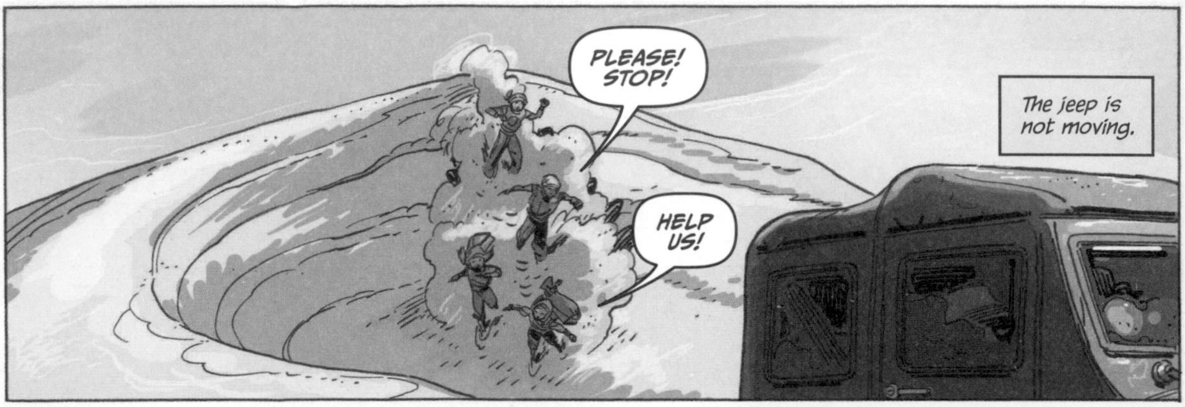
PLEASE! STOP!
The jeep is not moving.
HELP US!

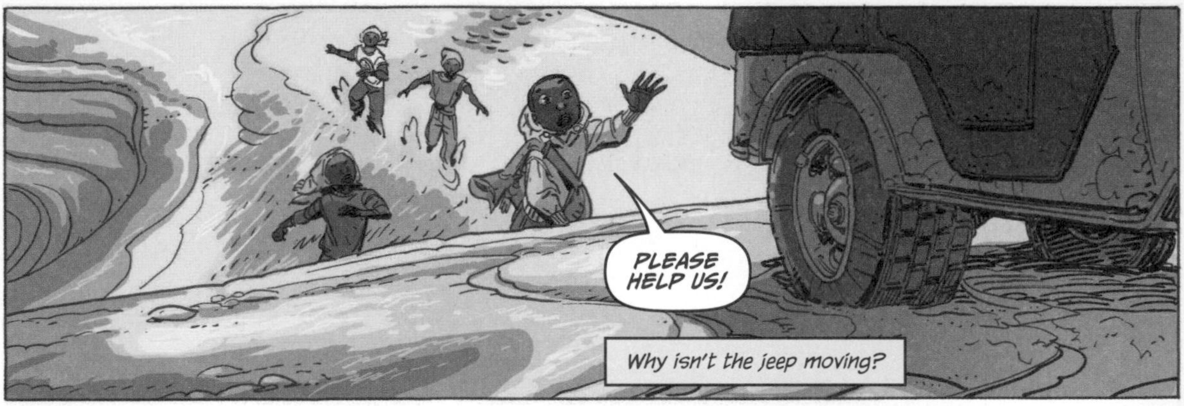
PLEASE HELP US!
Why isn't the jeep moving?

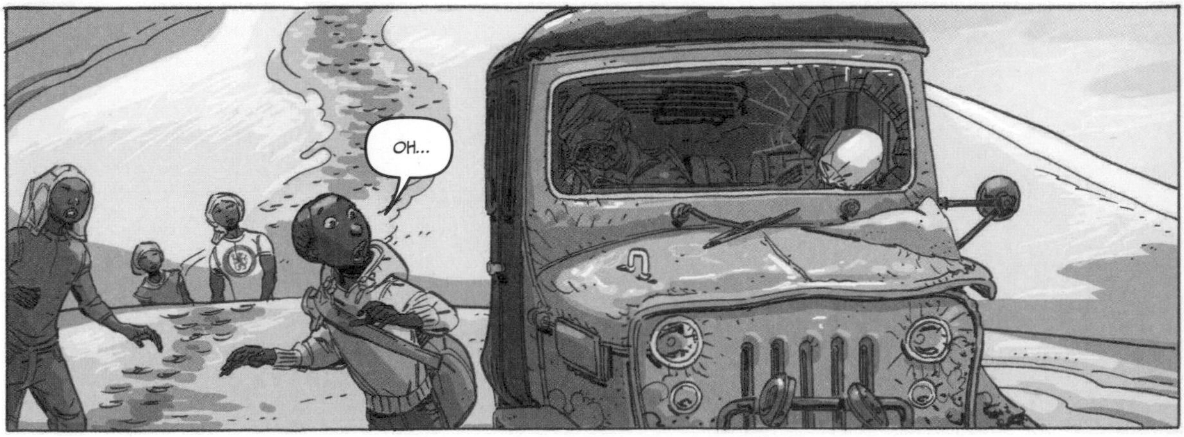
OH...

80

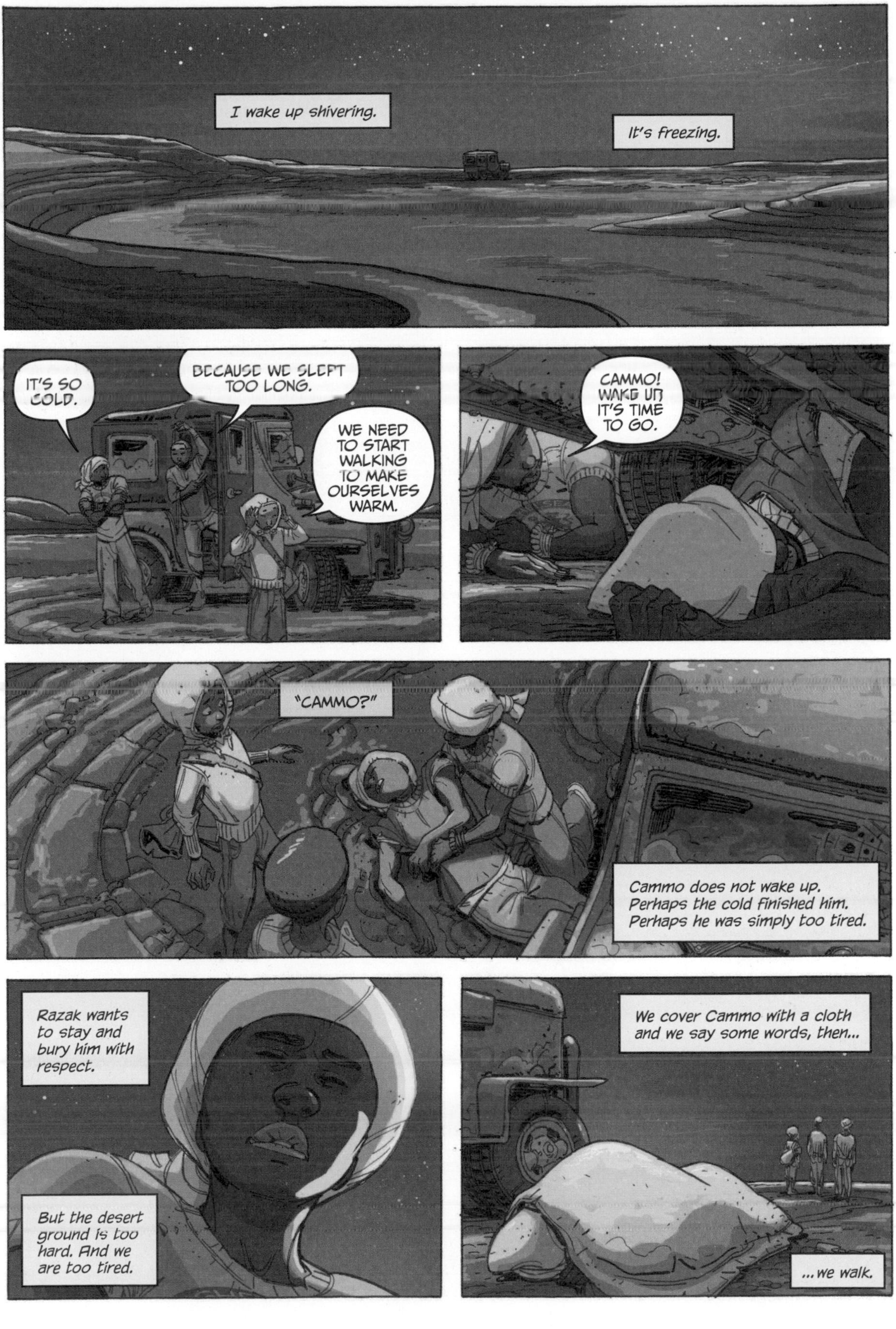
I wake up shivering.
It's freezing.
IT'S SO COLD.
BECAUSE WE SLEPT TOO LONG.
WE NEED TO START WALKING TO MAKE OURSELVES WARM.
CAMMO! WAKE UP. IT'S TIME TO GO.
"CAMMO?"
Cammo does not wake up. Perhaps the cold finished him. Perhaps he was simply too tired.
Razak wants to stay and bury him with respect.
But the desert ground is too hard. And we are too tired.
We cover Cammo with a cloth and we say some words, then...
...we walk.

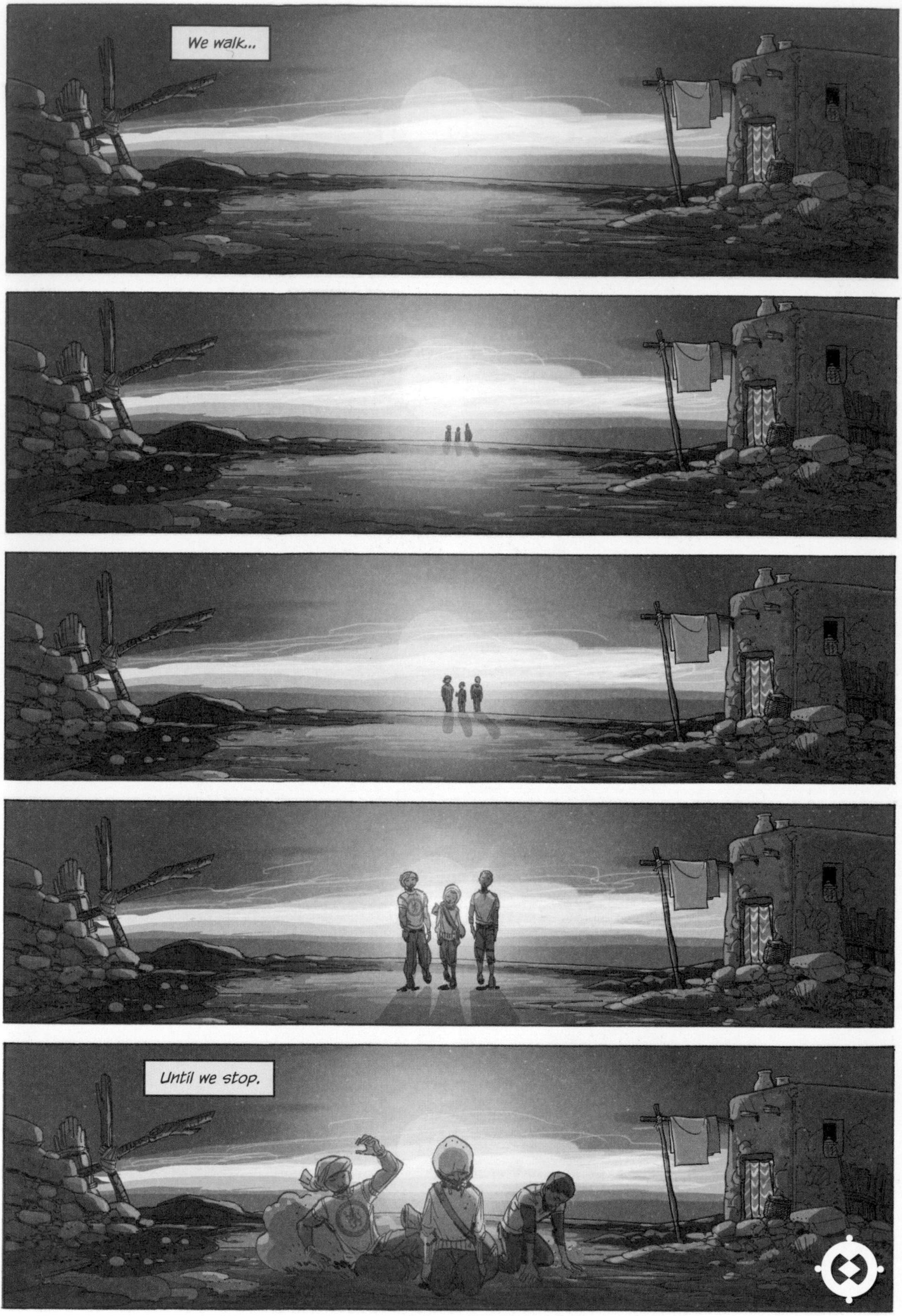
We walk...
Until we stop.

NOW

CHAPTER 13

Morning.

Everyone is hungry and thirsty.

Now all they want is land.

All any of us want is Europe.

Low clouds cover the sky ahead of us.

One of them has a heartbeat.

THUMP THUMP THUMP THUMP

The heartbeat gets louder...

Deeper...

Until it thuds in our chests and we see it...

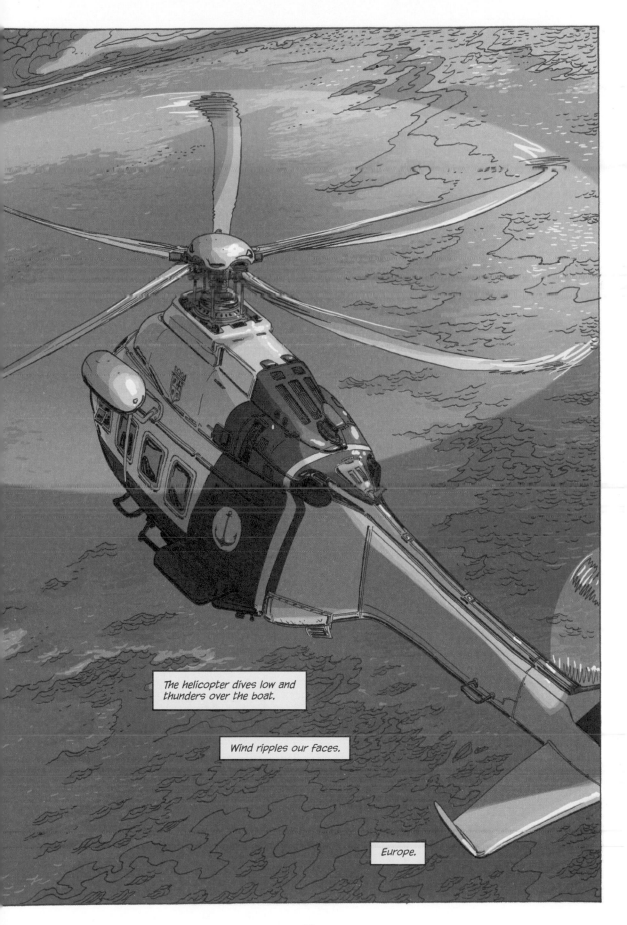

The helicopter dives low and thunders over the boat.

Wind ripples our faces.

Europe.

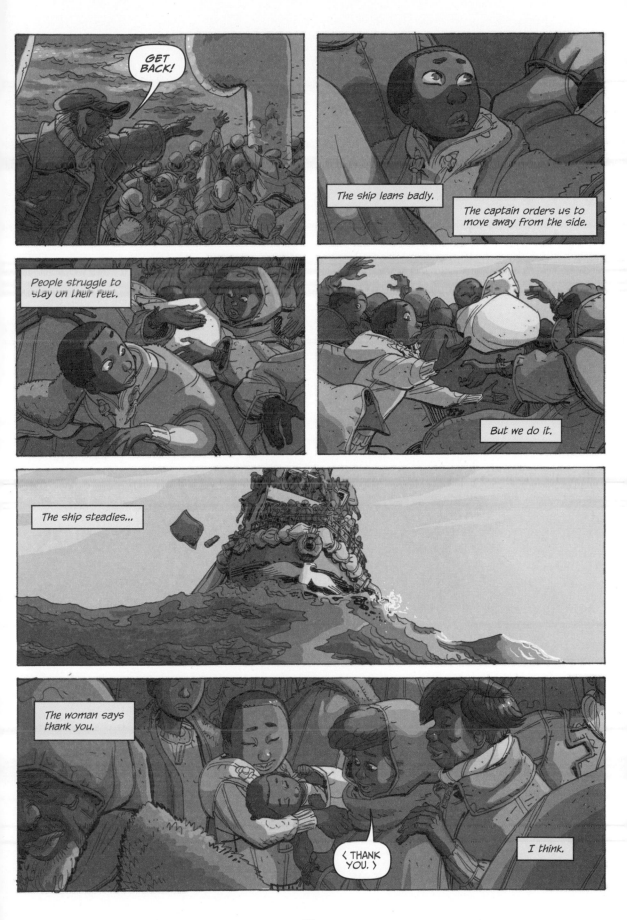

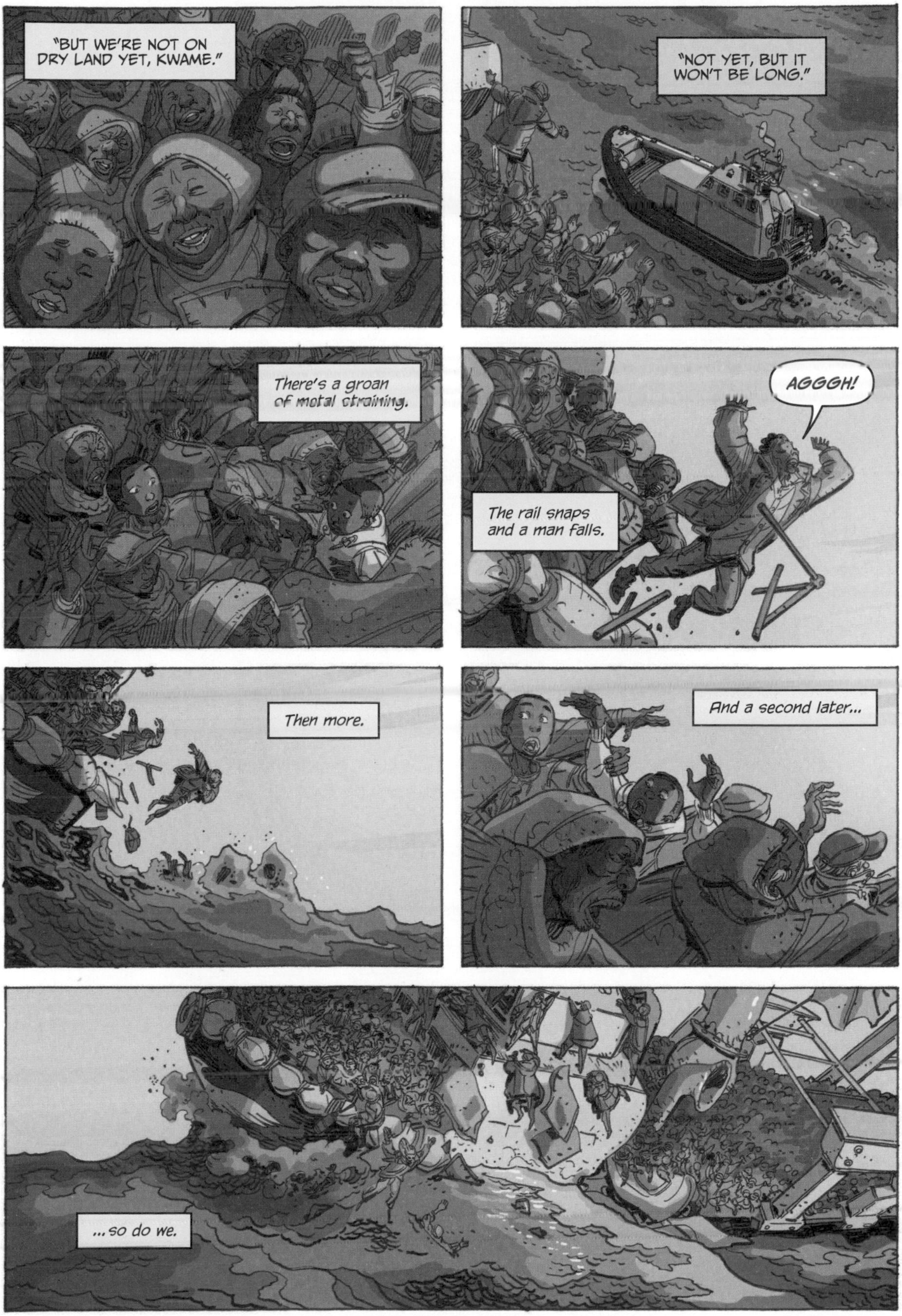
"BUT WE'RE NOT ON DRY LAND YET, KWAME."
"NOT YET, BUT IT WON'T BE LONG."
There's a groan of metal straining.
AGGGH!
The rail snaps and a man falls.
Then more.
And a second later...
...so do we.

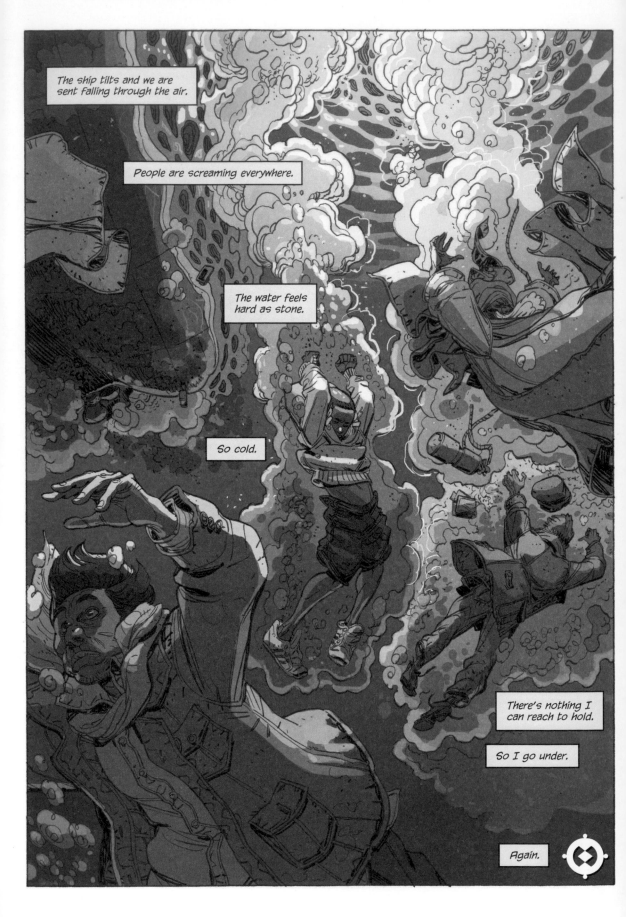

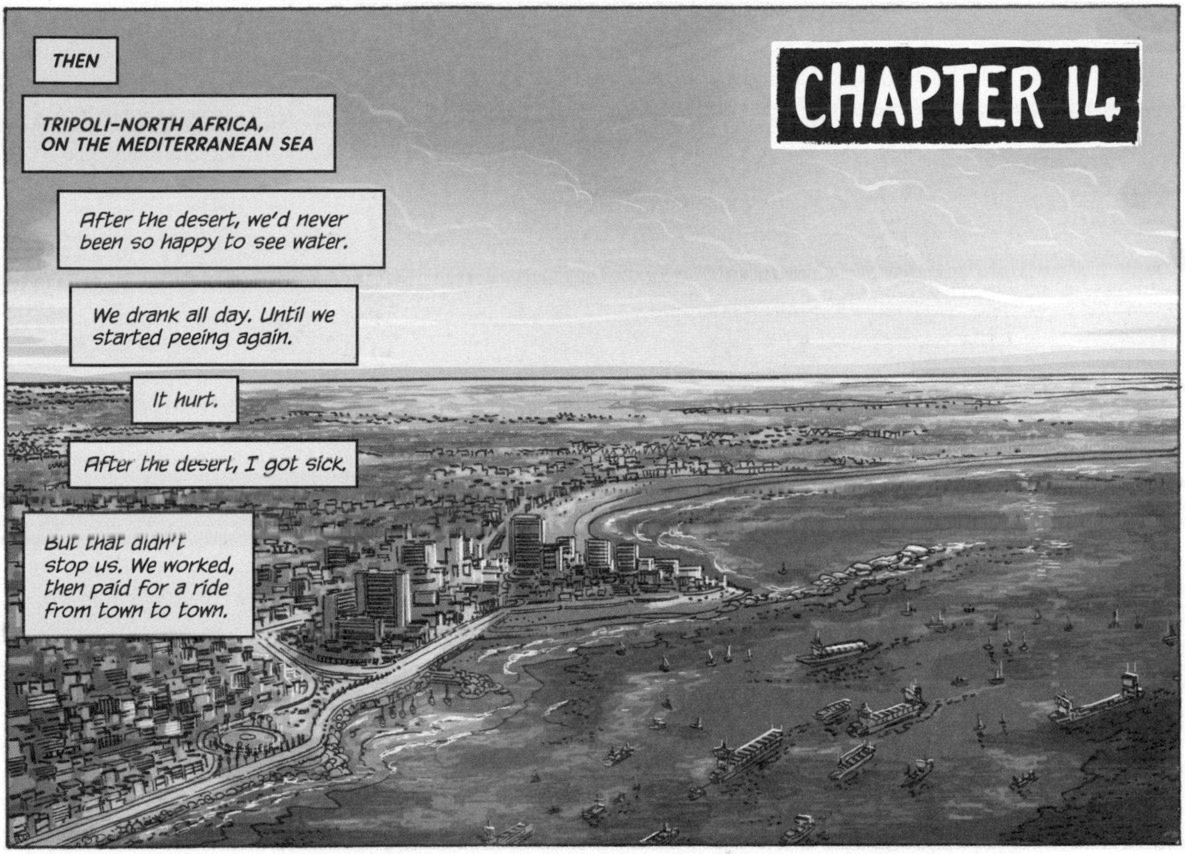
THEN
CHAPTER 14
TRIPOLI–NORTH AFRICA, ON THE MEDITERRANEAN SEA
After the desert, we'd never been so happy to see water.
We drank all day. Until we started peeing again.
It hurt.
After the desert, I got sick.
But that didn't stop us. We worked, then paid for a ride from town to town.

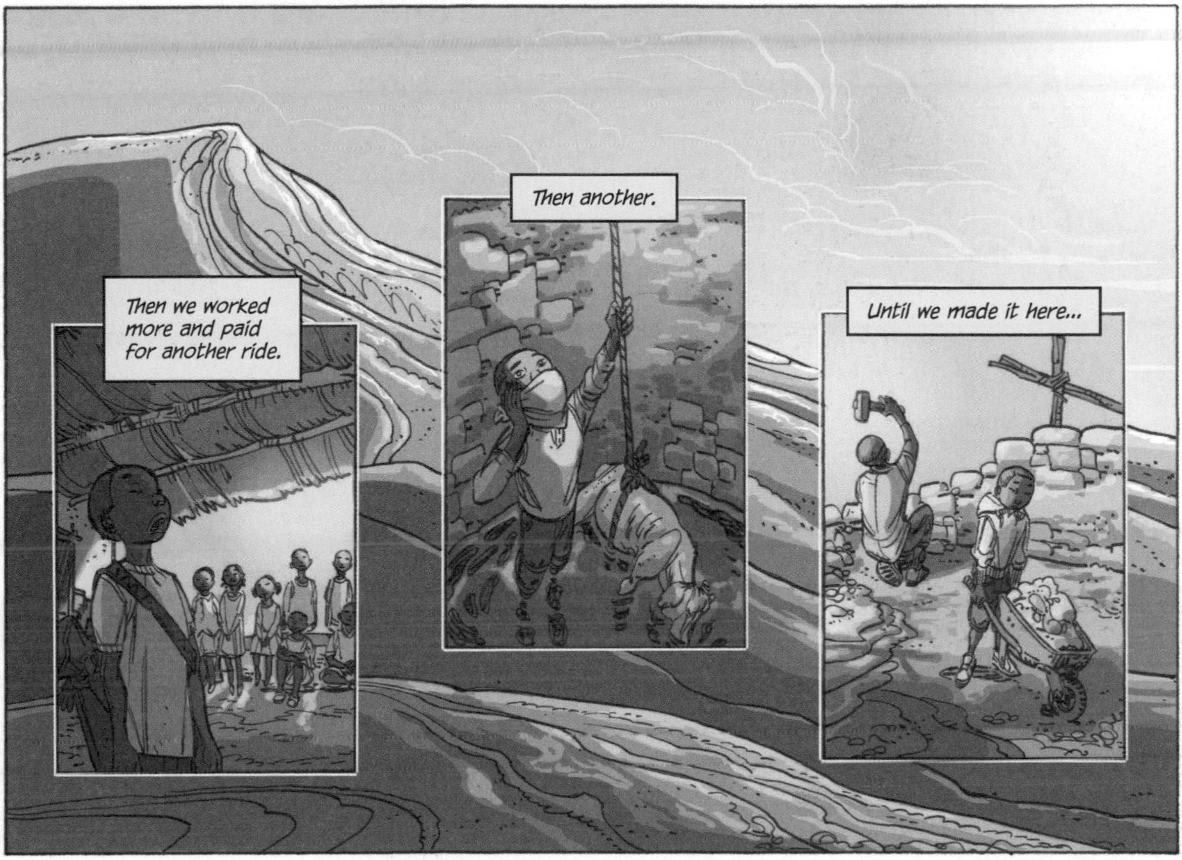
Then we worked more and paid for another ride.
Then another.
Until we made it here...

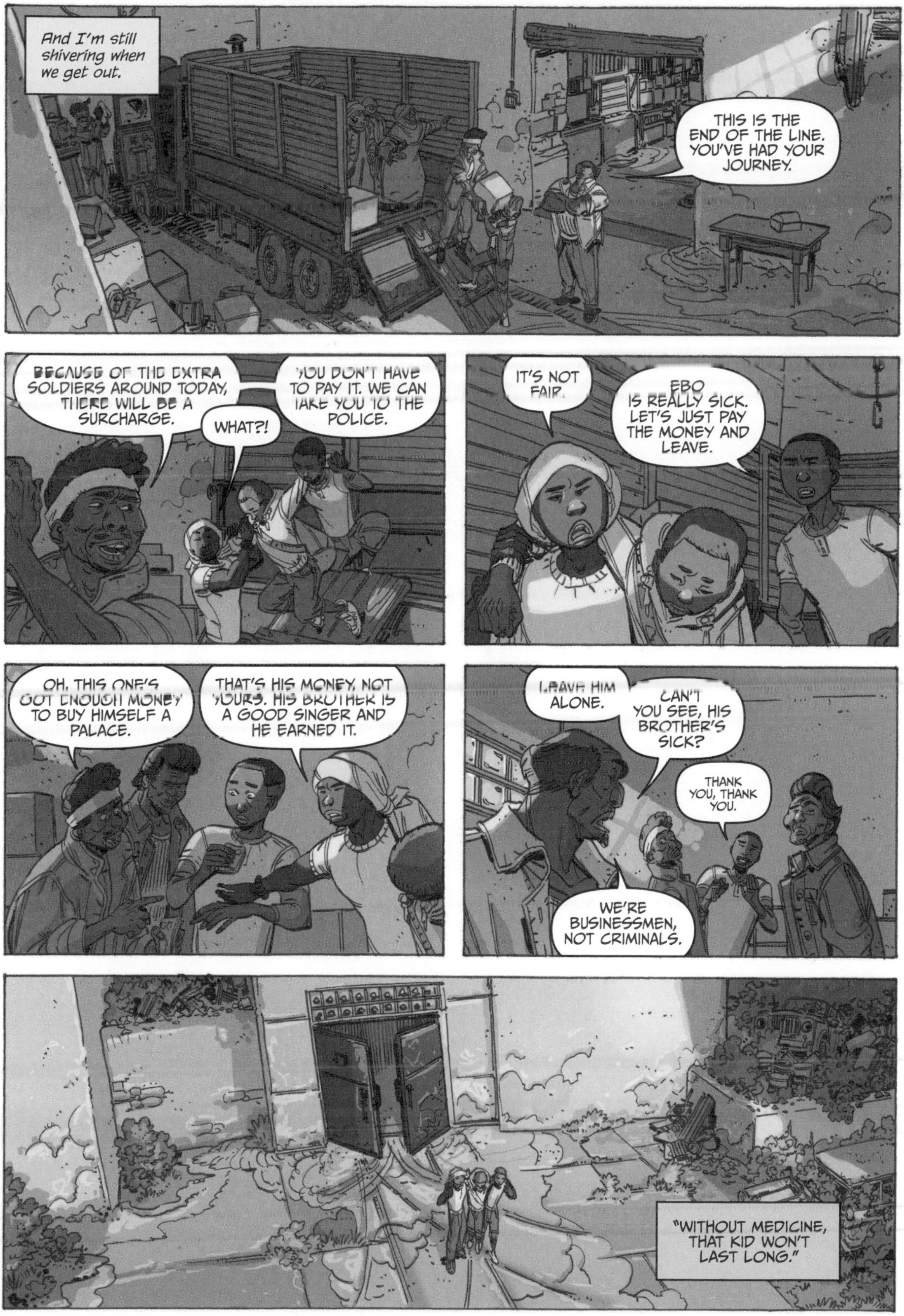

And I'm still shivering when we get out.
THIS IS THE END OF THE LINE. YOU'VE HAD YOUR JOURNEY.
BECAUSE OF THE EXTRA SOLDIERS AROUND TODAY, THERE WILL BE A SURCHARGE.
WHAT?!
YOU DON'T HAVE TO PAY IT. WE CAN TAKE YOU TO THE POLICE.
IT'S NOT FAIR.
EBO IS REALLY SICK. LET'S JUST PAY THE MONEY AND LEAVE.
OH, THIS ONE'S GOT ENOUGH MONEY TO BUY HIMSELF A PALACE.
THAT'S HIS MONEY, NOT YOURS. HIS BROTHER IS A GOOD SINGER AND HE EARNED IT.
LEAVE HIM ALONE.
CAN'T YOU SEE, HIS BROTHER'S SICK?
THANK YOU, THANK YOU.
WE'RE BUSINESSMEN, NOT CRIMINALS.
"WITHOUT MEDICINE, THAT KID WON'T LAST LONG."

KWAME?

THERE WERE RATS ALL OVER HIM. HE'S GETTING WORSE.

I HAVE TO GET EBO TO A HOSPITAL.

KWAME, IF YOU GO INTO A HOSPITAL YOU CAN GET CAUGHT WITHOUT PAPERS AND ARRESTED.

I FOUND MY FRIEND. THIS IS NURU.

HE HAS A FRIEND WHO HAS A FRIEND THAT GOT HIM MEDICINE.

STOLEN MEDICINE?

IT MIGHT CURE HIS FEVER.

TAKING STOLEN MEDICINE IS NOT GOOD.

THE WRONG PILLS CAN KILL.

"HE'S YOUR BROTHER. IT'S YOUR CHOICE, KWAME. IT'S UP TO YOU."

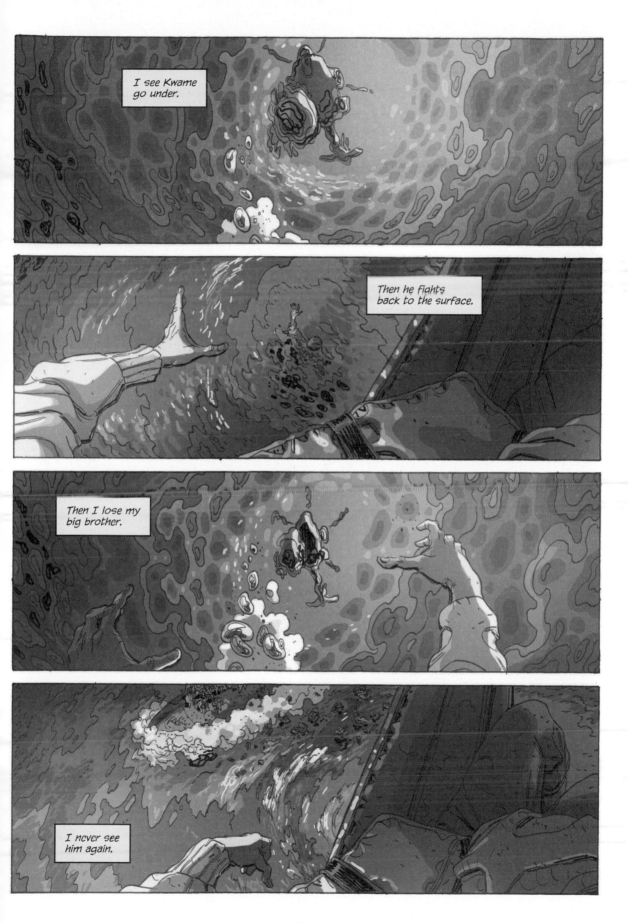

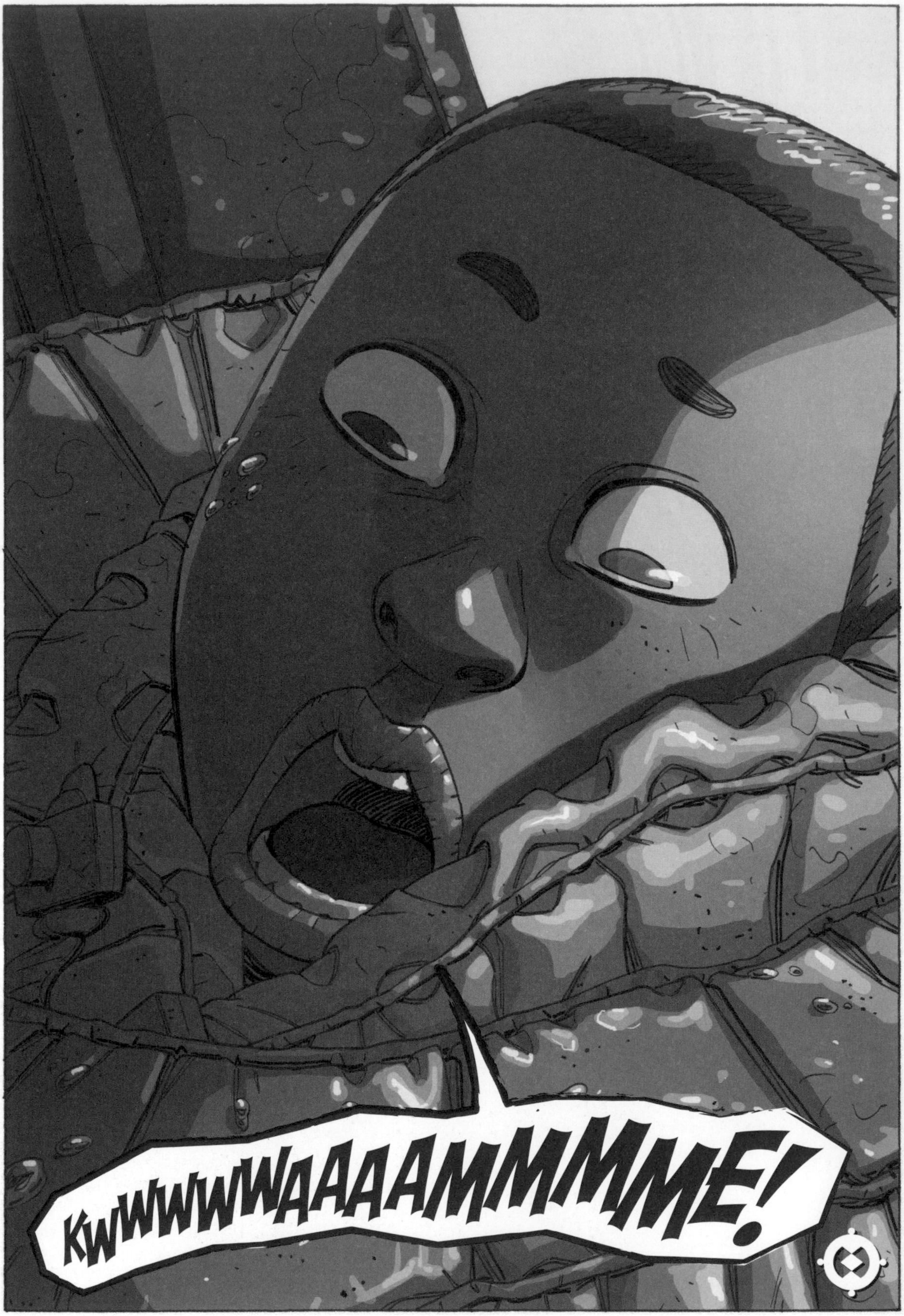
KWWWWWAAAAMMMMME!

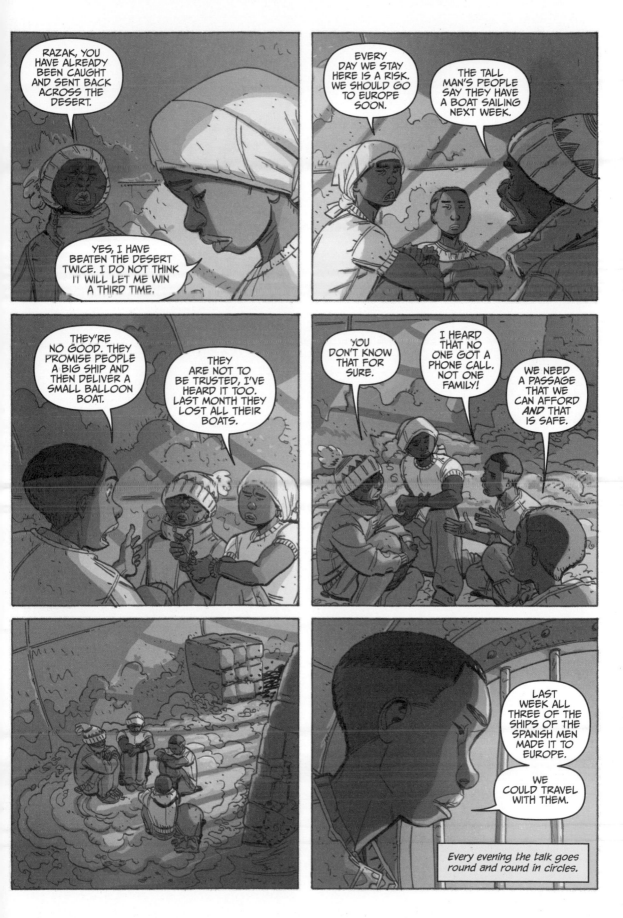

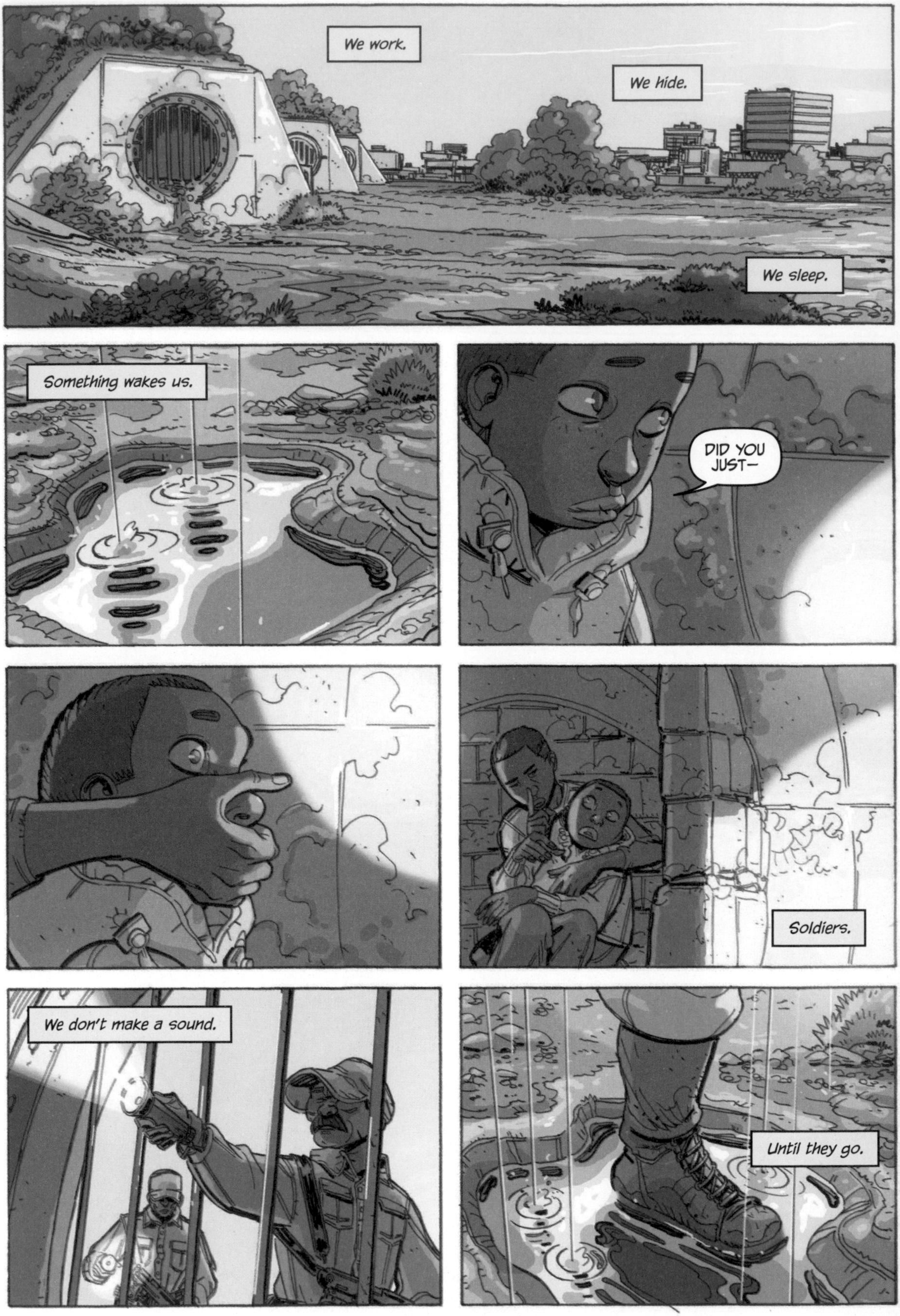
We work.
We hide.
We sleep.
Something wakes us.
DID YOU JUST—
Soldiers.
We don't make a sound.
Until they go.

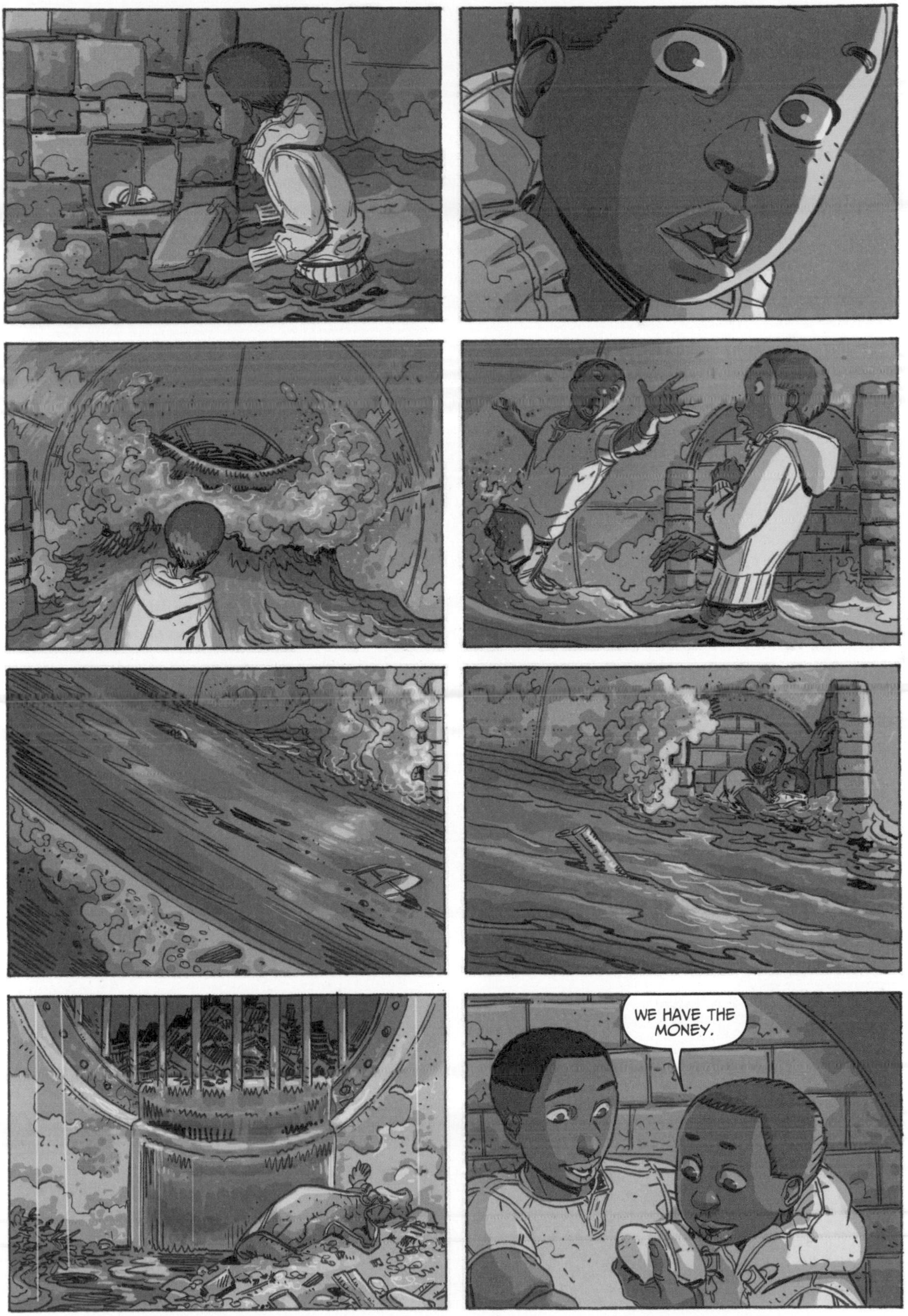
WE HAVE THE MONEY.

114

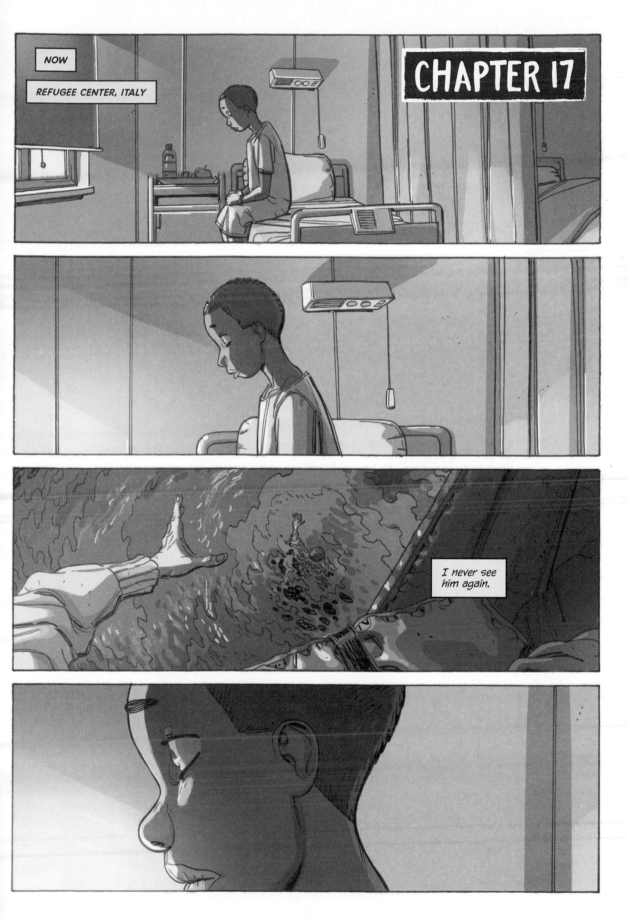

NOW

REFUGEE CENTER, ITALY

CHAPTER 17

I never see him again.

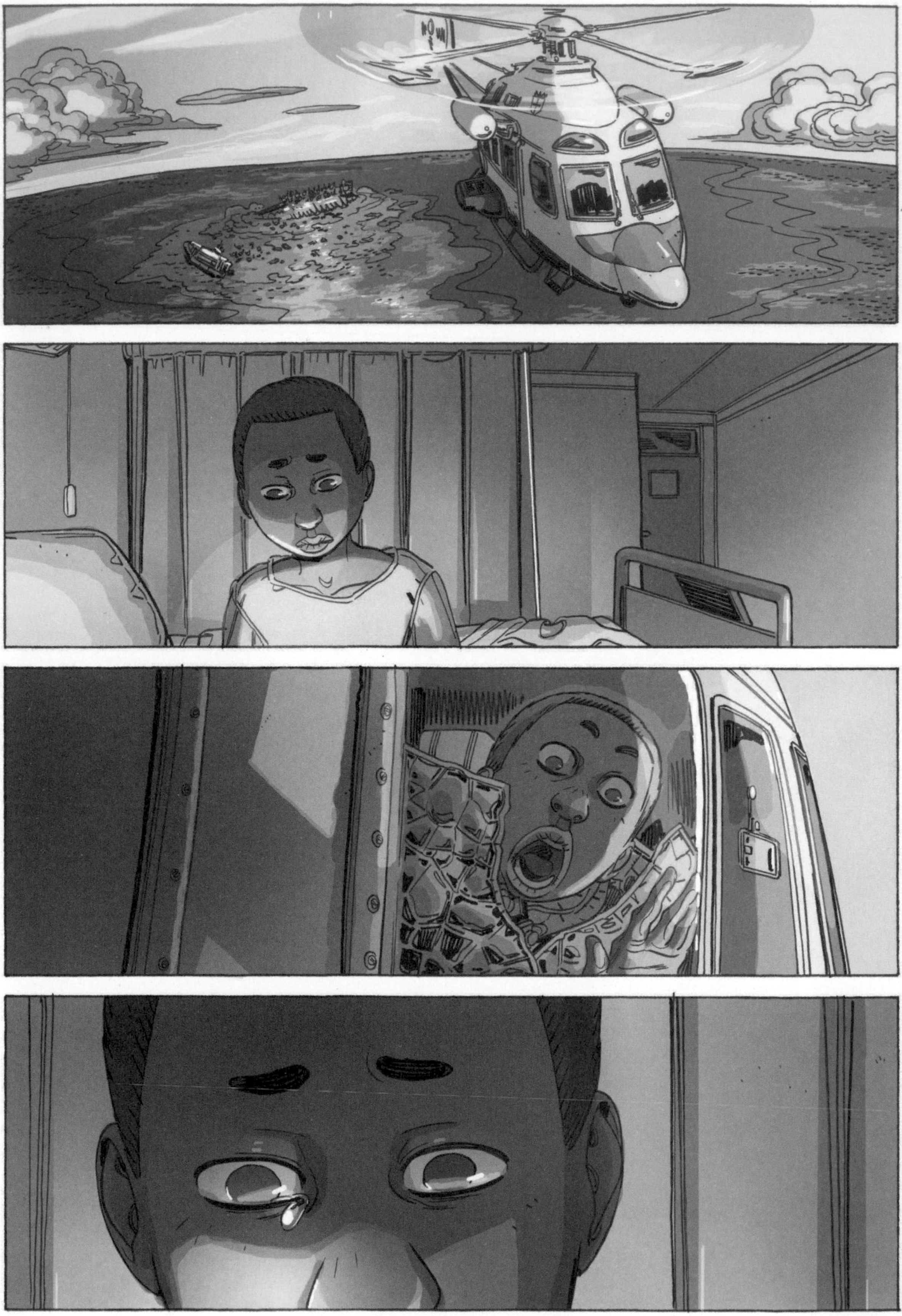

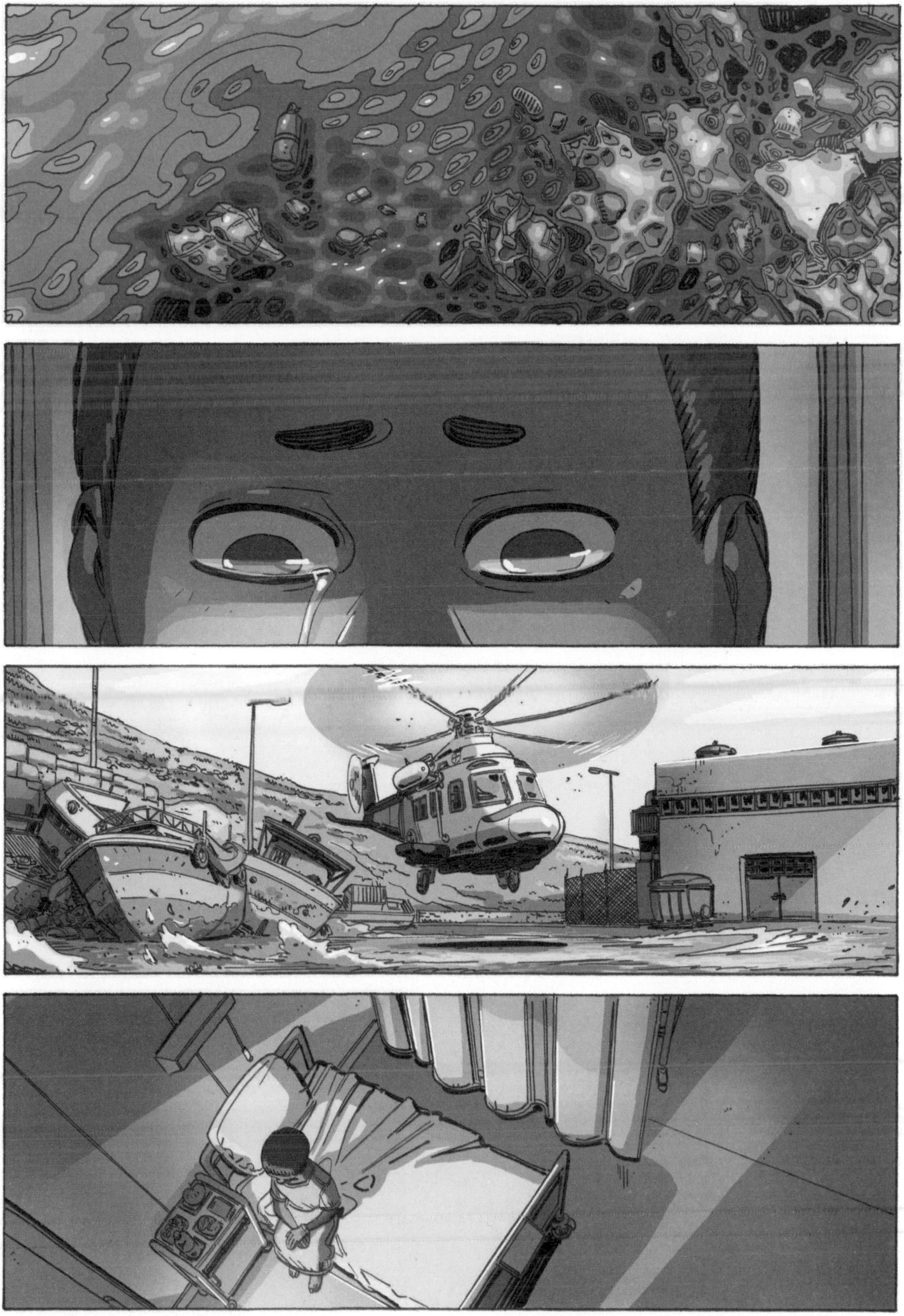

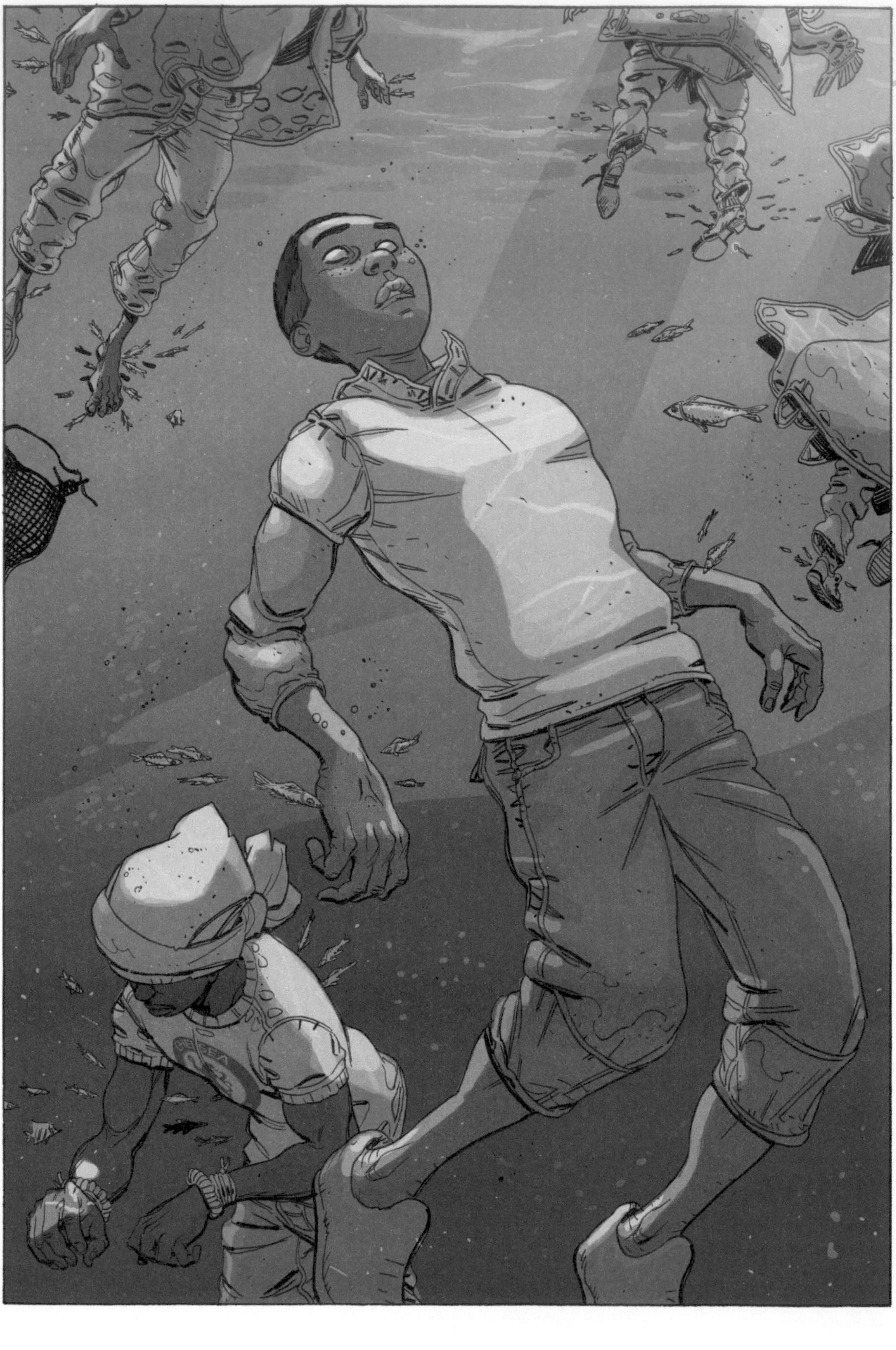

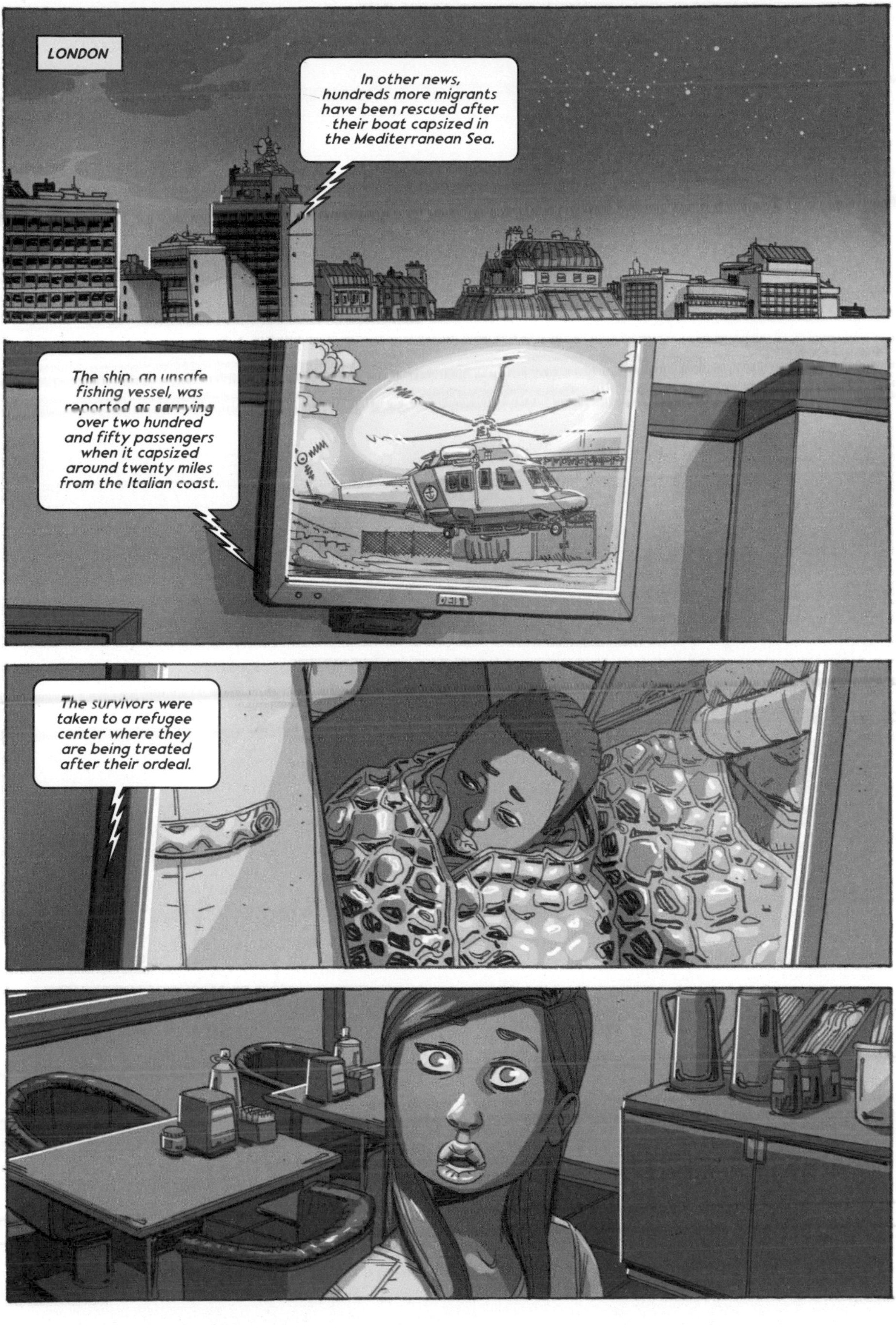
LONDON
In other news, hundreds more migrants have been rescued after their boat capsized in the Mediterranean Sea.
The ship, an unsafe fishing vessel, was reported as carrying over two hundred and fifty passengers when it capsized around twenty miles from the Italian coast.
The survivors were taken to a refugee center where they are being treated after their ordeal.

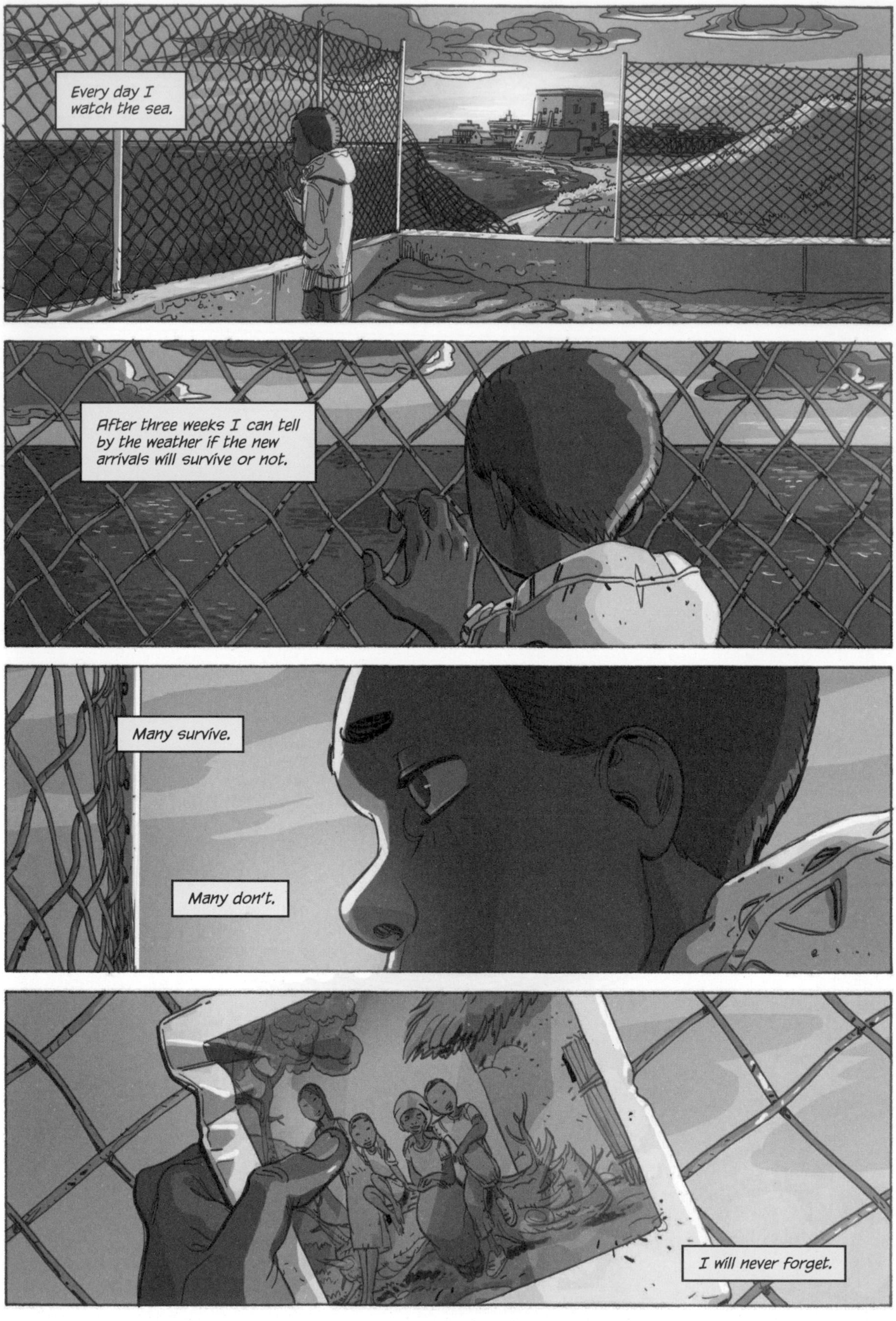
Every day I watch the sea.
After three weeks I can tell by the weather if the new arrivals will survive or not.
Many survive.
Many don't.
I will never forget.

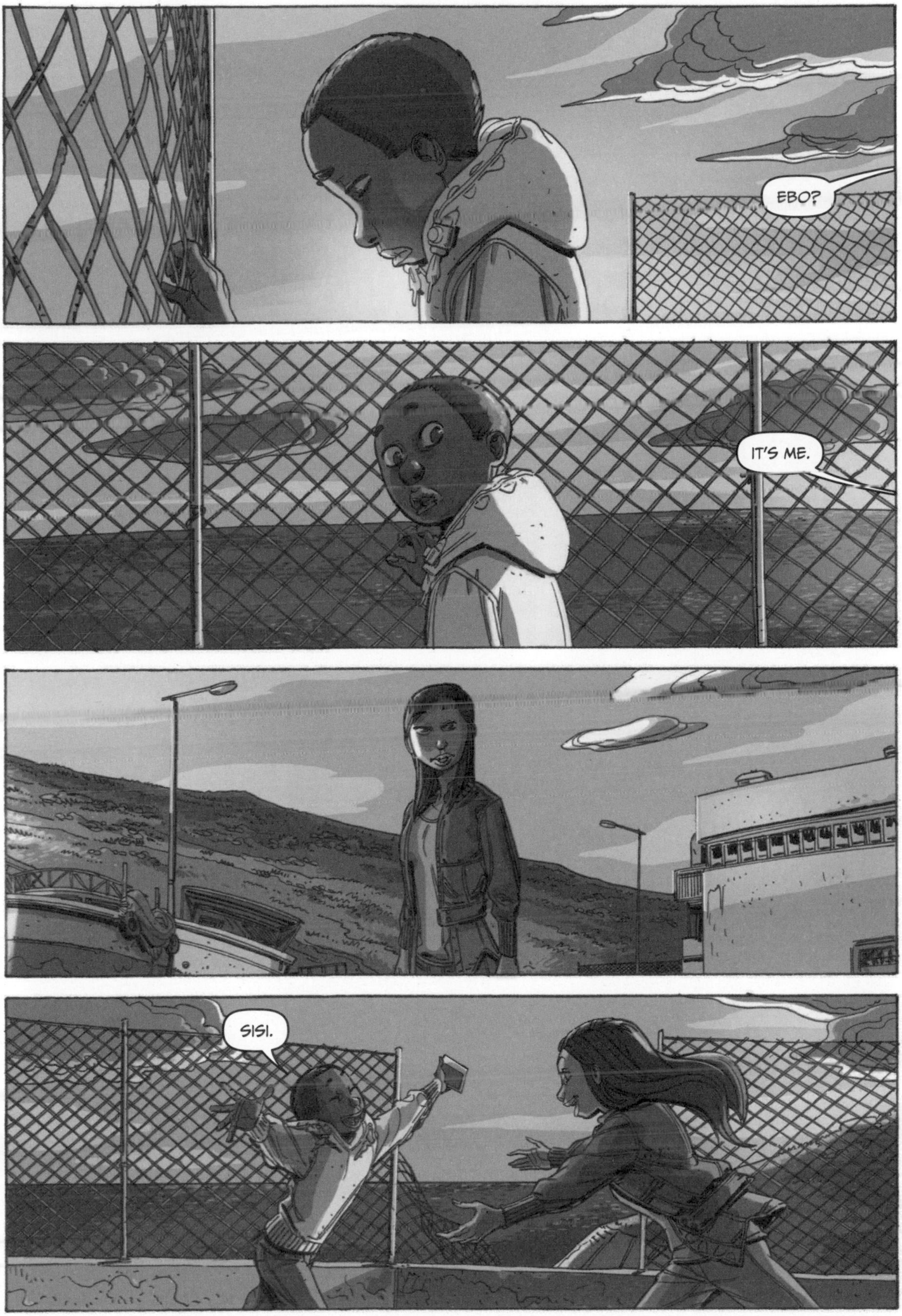
EBO?
IT'S ME.
SISI.

EBO'S JOURNEY

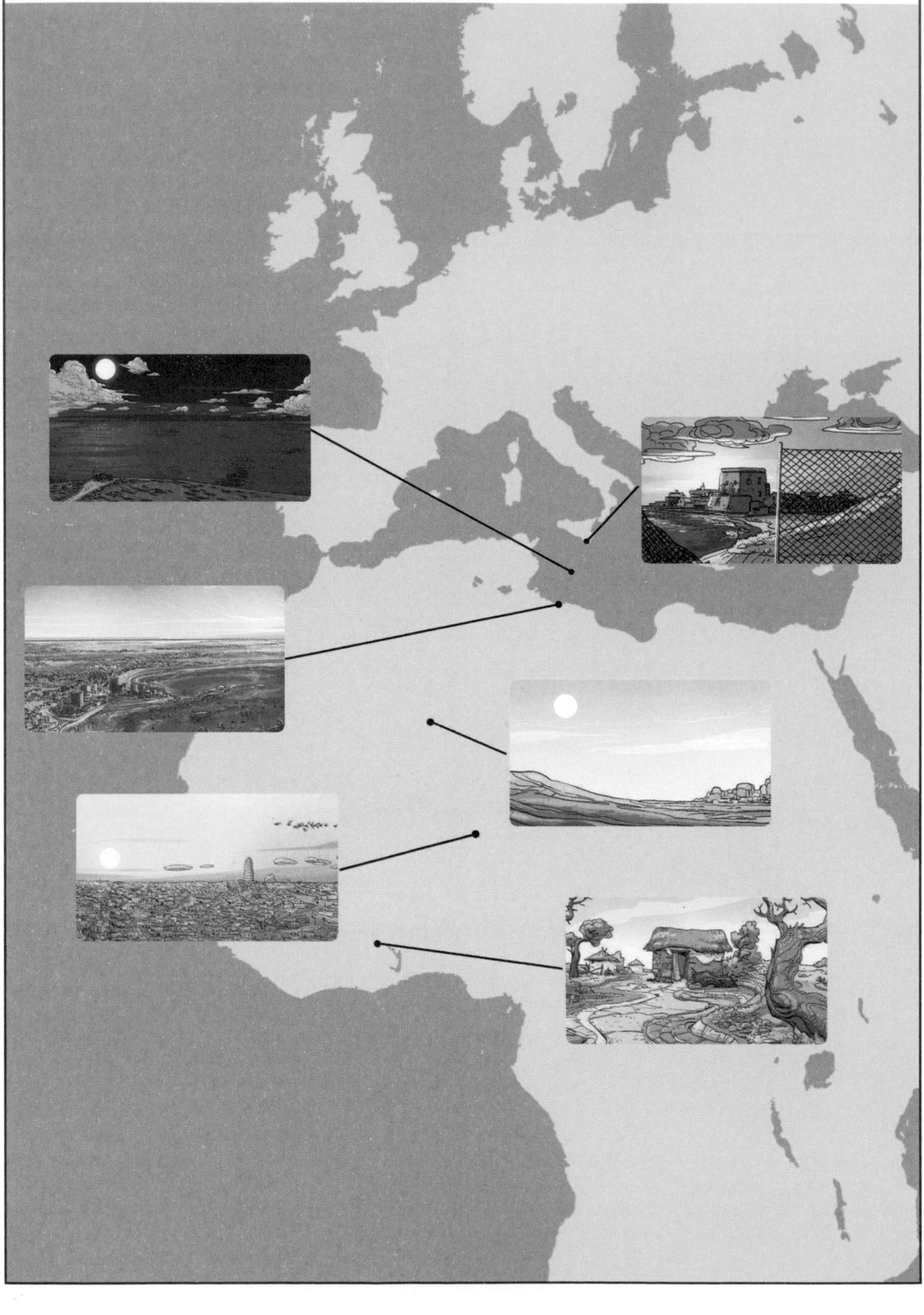

CREATORS' NOTE

The story you've just read about Ebo's journey is a work of fiction, but every separate element of it is true.

Every year, many thousands of men, women, and children risk their lives by trying to make the dangerous three-hundred-mile sea crossing between Northern Africa and Italy. They pay large sums of money to smugglers who in return provide poorly prepared, unseaworthy boats. The distances involved are formidable and the sea currents are unpredictable. The smuggling networks that run these operations make fortunes with no regard for human life. They send their victims out to sea in death traps.

Many innocents die as a result, their loss of life often unknown and unrecorded. In 2015, more than a million migrants crossed the Mediterranean Sea to enter Europe. The United Nations has described the situation as a "colossal humanitarian catastrophe" and it is still going on.

The migrants come from different countries and travel for different reasons. Some are refugees fleeing war-torn countries like Syria. Others, like Ebo, are following family members seeking a new life with better opportunities in Europe.

Most of the people trying to cross the Mediterranean Sea have already endured a long and dangerous journey. Crossing the Sahara Desert is just as dangerous as crossing the Mediterranean Sea. Broken trucks and broken promises mean many migrants lose their lives in the desert sands. Many more migrants would perish in the Mediterranean without the daily search-and-rescue operations run by humanitarian organizations.

It's not a journey to be undertaken lightly. Every person making the choice to embark on that journey has their own reasons for doing so. And every person is a human being.

Eoin Colfer
Andrew Donkin
Giovanni Rigano

JOURNEY: HELEN'S STORY

WORDS BY HELEN AS TOLD TO WOMEN FOR REFUGEE WOMEN

ADAPTED FOR COMICS BY COLFER/DONKIN/RIGANO

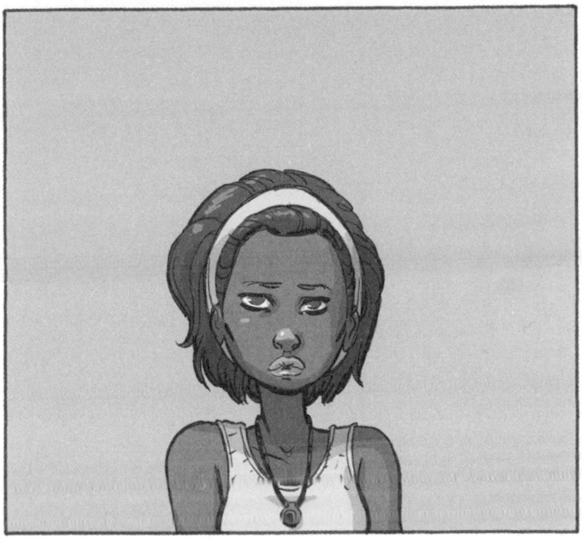

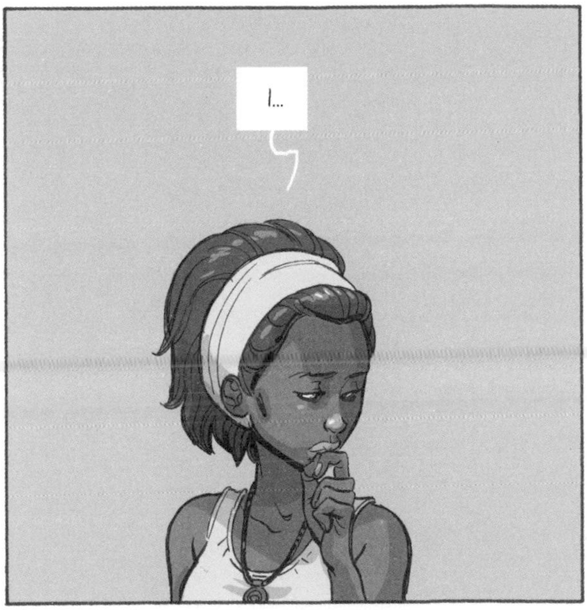
I...

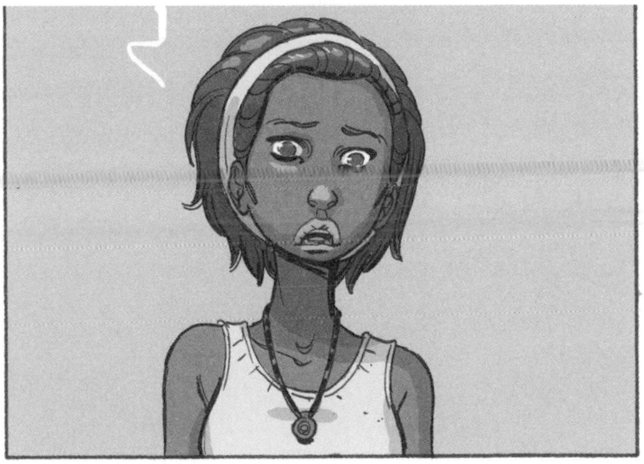
I AM HELEN.
I WAS BORN IN ERITREA. MY MOTHER DIED WHEN I WAS YOUNG. MY FAMILY WERE SPLIT AND MY FATHER HAD TO FLEE. AT THE AGE OF THIRTEEN, I WENT TO SUDAN TO LOOK FOR HIM AND ENDED UP STAYING THERE MANY YEARS.

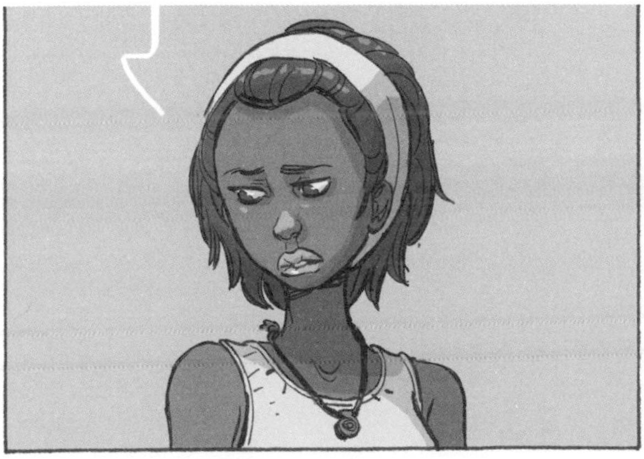
I LIVED IN HIDING, BECAUSE I DIDN'T HAVE ANY PAPERS. AN ELDERLY ETHIOPIAN WOMAN TOOK ME IN. I WORKED FOR HER MANY YEARS WITHOUT PAY BUT LAST YEAR SHE TOLD ME I HAD TO LEAVE.

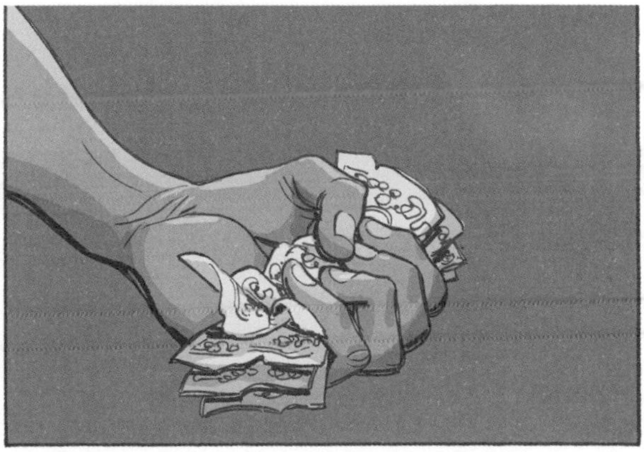
"SHE KNEW SOME TRAFFICKERS WHO SAID THEY WOULD TAKE ME THROUGH THE DESERT, THROUGH LIBYA, AND ACROSS THE SEA TO ITALY, AND SHE MADE THE FIRST PAYMENT FOR ME."

"WE CROSSED THE SAHARA DESERT IN A TRUCK, TRAVELING DAY AND NIGHT FOR FIFTEEN DAYS. IT WAS SO SANDY AND HOT."

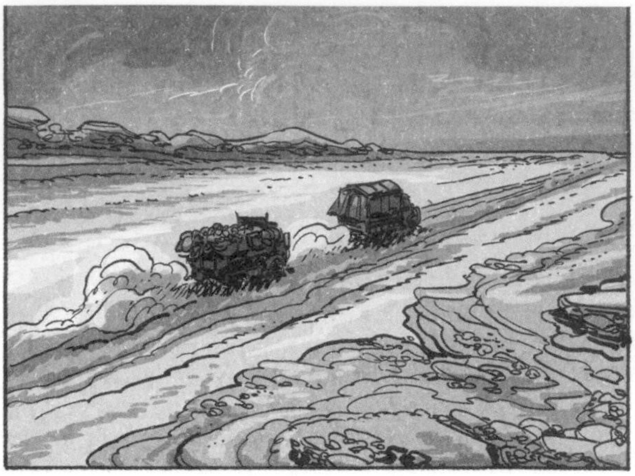

"WE HAD BROUGHT FOOD AND WATER AND WE THOUGHT WE HAD WHAT WE NEEDED. THEN THE TRUCK BROKE DOWN. THERE WAS NO SHADE—WE WERE BURNT BY THE SUN, AND THE CONSTANT HEAT MADE US MORE AND MORE THIRSTY."

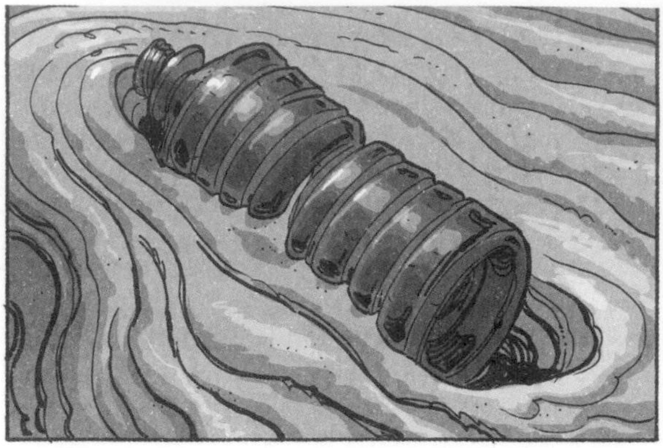

ONE MAN LOST HIS BROTHER, AND A WOMAN I HAD KNOWN IN SUDAN ALSO DIED.

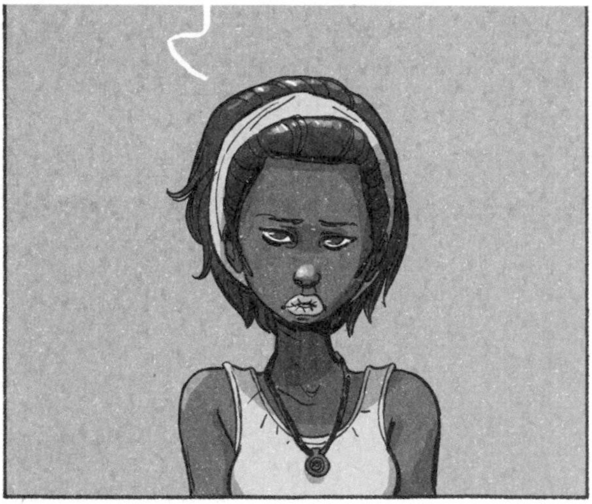

"WE TRIED TO BURY OUR FRIENDS. THE MEN DUG AND WE WOMEN WEPT. THOSE FRIENDS OF OURS WERE BURIED IN A SHALLOW GRAVE—IT WASN'T REALLY A BURIAL. THE SAND WILL NOT COVER THEM LONG."

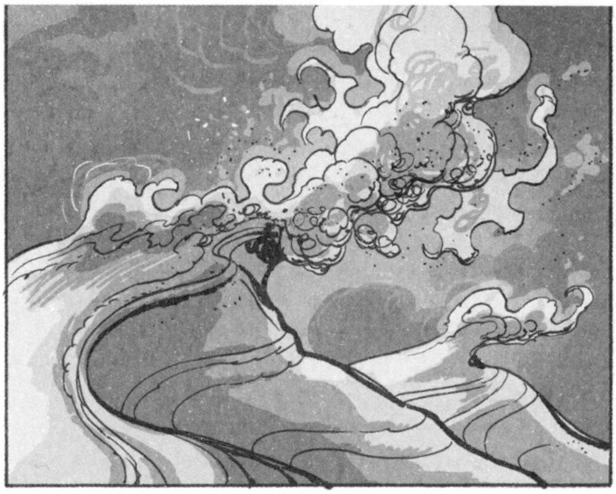

"WHEN ANOTHER TRUCK CAME FOR US IN THE DESERT, WE THOUGHT WE WERE BEING SAVED, BUT THESE MEN WERE TRAFFICKERS TOO."

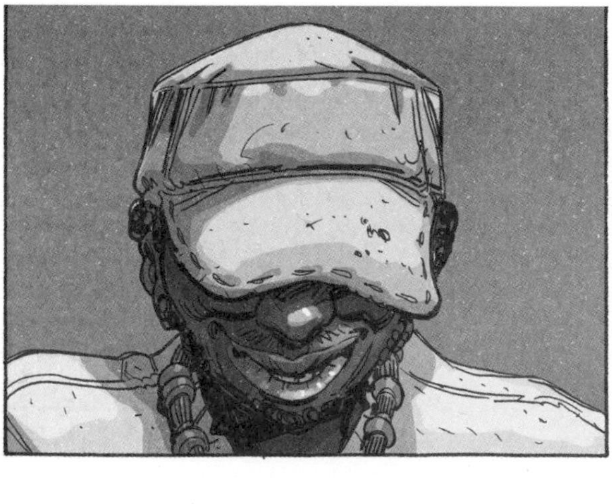

THEY TOOK US TO LIBYA, WHICH WAS GOOD, BUT THEN THEY LOCKED US UP AND DEMANDED MONEY OR WE WOULD DIE.

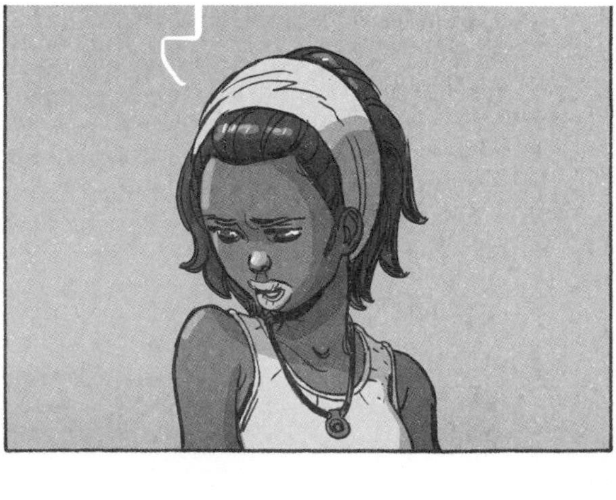

"THEY GAVE ENOUGH FOOD SO WE WOULDN'T DIE, BUT NOT MUCH—WE WERE ALWAYS IN THE BALANCE BETWEEN LIFE AND DEATH."

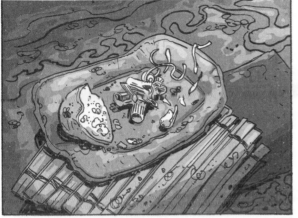

I THOUGHT I WOULD NEVER MAKE IT OUT OF THAT PRISON, BECAUSE I HAD NO FAMILY I COULD CALL ON TO SEND MONEY FOR ME TO BE RELEASED.

"BUT MY FELLOW PRISONERS SAVED ME. WHEN THEY WERE ASKING THEIR FAMILIES TO SAVE THEM FROM THE PRISON, THEY ALSO ASKED FOR EXTRA MONEY TO GET ME OUT OF THERE."

WHEN WE SAILED, WE WERE LUCKY.

"THE BOAT BEHIND US, WHICH HAD OVER FOUR HUNDRED PEOPLE IN IT, SANK. I KNEW SOME OF THE PEOPLE ON THERE."

"BUT THE ITALIAN COAST GUARDS MET OUR BOAT AND TOOK US TO ITALY. A COUPLE OF THE PEOPLE I WAS WITH SAID THAT THEY WERE TRAVELING ON TO FRANCE TO TRY TO GET TO THE UK, AND ASKED ME IF I WANTED TO JOIN THEM."

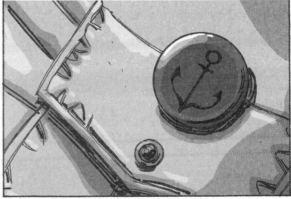

"I WENT TO ISBERGUES, A CAMP NEAR TO CALAIS, AND LIVED THERE FOR TWO MONTHS. I WAS DESPERATE TO REACH A SAFE PLACE FOR ME. LIFE WAS HARD. BY NOW, I KNEW I WAS PREGNANT."

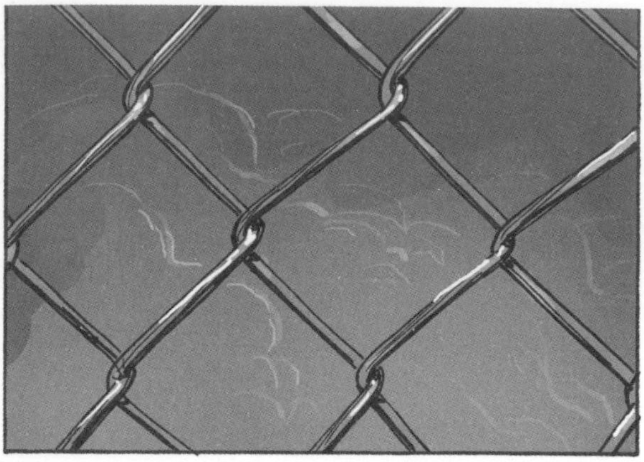

THERE WERE NO TOILETS, NO SHOWERS. FIVE OF US ON ONE MATTRESS. THERE WAS NO SLEEP BECAUSE DURING THE DAY PEOPLE WOULD COME AND GO, AND AT NIGHT I WOULD ALWAYS BE OUT TRYING TO GET ON THE TRUCKS.

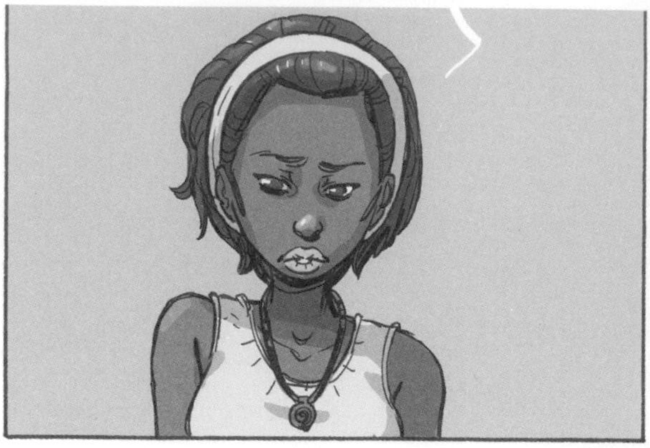

"BUT THERE WAS ONLY ONE THING ON MY MIND— THAT IF I GOT TO THE UK I WOULD REACH A SAFE PLACE WHERE I AND MY BABY COULD HAVE A GOOD CHANCE AT LIFE. I WAS DETERMINED TO GET HERE. I TRIED EVERY NIGHT WITHOUT FAIL."

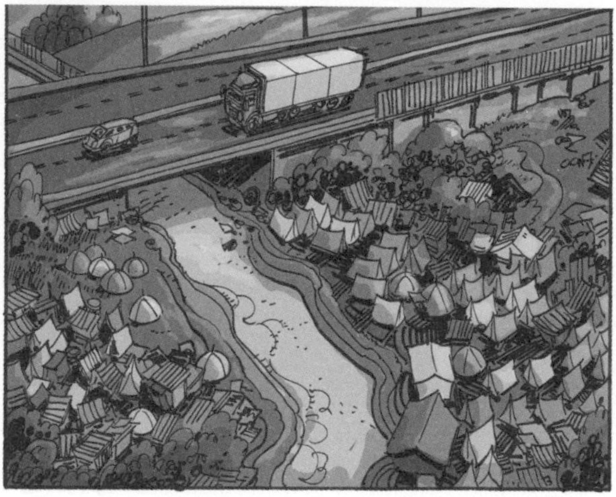

"SO I CAME TO THIS COUNTRY HIDING IN A TRUCK. THIRTY PEOPLE BROKE INTO THE SAME ONE AND HID. AT THE BORDER, THE TRUCK WAS SEARCHED AND THE OTHER TWENTY-NINE PEOPLE WERE FOUND AND HAD TO GET OFF."

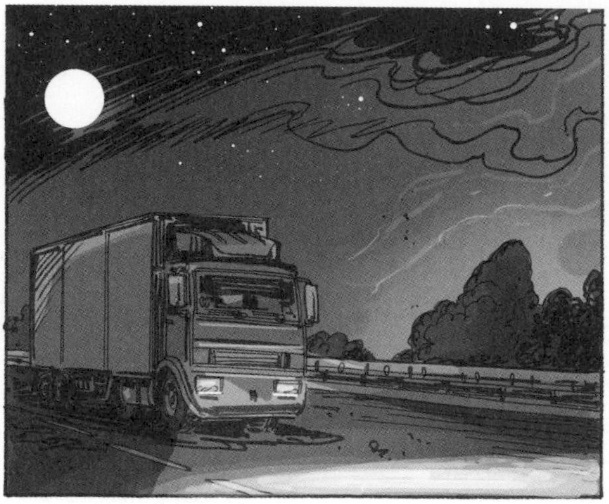

"I WAS UNDER THE FLOORING SO THEY COULDN'T FIND ME. UNKNOWINGLY, THE POLICE WERE WALKING ON TOP OF ME."

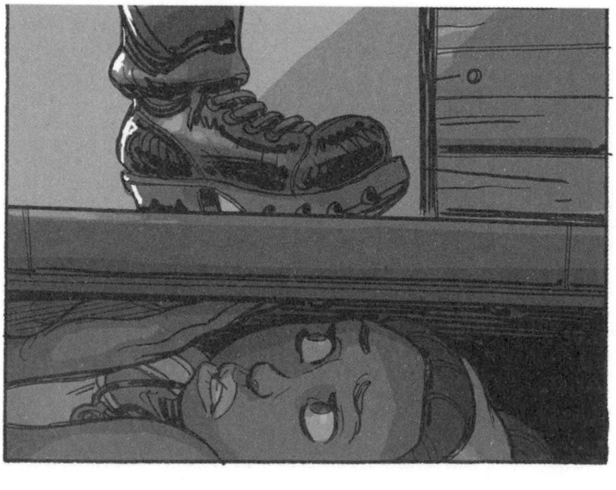

WHEN THE TRUCK STOPPED I GOT UP AND KNEW THERE WAS SOMETHING WRONG.

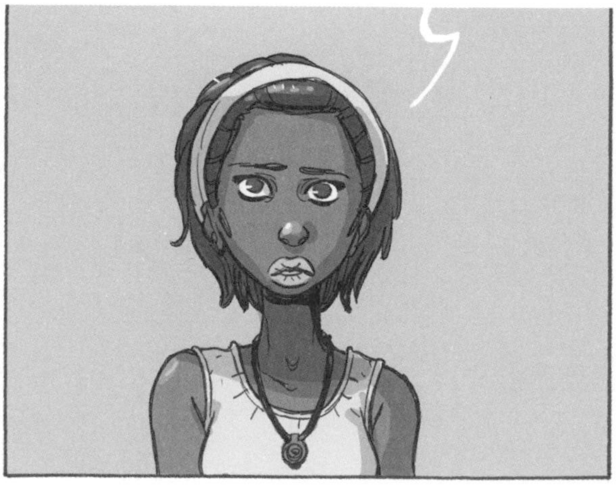

"I WAS IN PAIN."

"THE TRUCK DRIVER SHOUTED AT ME WHEN HE SAW ME, AND SAID HE COULDN'T DO ANYTHING TO HELP."

"THE POLICE TOOK ME TO THE HOSPITAL, BUT I HAD LOST MY BABY."

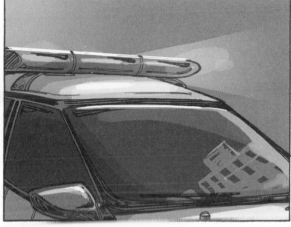

"NOW, I LIVE IN A HOSTEL IN LEEDS. I AM GIVEN MEALS BUT I DO NOT GET ANY MONEY AND I AM NOT ALLOWED TO WORK. I AM NOT COMPLAINING BECAUSE I HAVE BEEN IN SITUATIONS THAT WERE MUCH WORSE."

EVEN THOUGH I PASSED THROUGH ALL THAT SUFFERING, I AM HERE NOW, AND I AM THANKFUL FOR THAT.

I WANT TO BE EDUCATED. I DIDN'T HAVE MUCH OPPORTUNITY FOR LEARNING IN MY COUNTRY. I STOPPED GOING TO SCHOOL WHEN I WAS TWELVE. I HOPE I CAN STUDY, BUT NOW I HAVE BECOME FORGETFUL. I DON'T REMEMBER THINGS. HOPEFULLY MY HEAD WILL START WORKING BETTER.

I WOULD LIKE TO BECOME A NURSE.

END

ACKNOWLEDGMENTS

Research consultant: Vivien Francis

Grateful thanks to all the people who have given their time and energy and knowledge to help with this book, especially:

Jo Adkins
Roberto Barrera
Sheila Brand
Jax Burgoyne
Paul Chapman
Miles Dennison
Jean Donkin
Peter Donkin
Mike Fillis
Jamie Finch
Ron Fogelman
Dr. Thomas Giddens
Sophie Hicks
Matthew Pennycook MP
Moe Redish
Antonio Scricco
Will Vunderink
Sarah Williams

The Estate of Elie Wiesel

Our lovely team at Hodder:
Anne McNeil
Alison Padley
Rachel Wade

The staff at the Caird Library & Archive at the National Maritime Museum, Greenwich, London, England.

Special thanks to all the people who talked to us about their experiences but who wished to remain anonymous.

And a huge thank you to the following individuals and their London-based charities:

Anne Stoltenberg and Nazek Ramadan at Migrant Voice
www.migrantvoice.org

Natasha Walter and Marchu Girma at Women for Refugee Women
www.RefugeeWomen.co.uk

Helen Mead at Greenwich Migrant Hub
www.greenwichmigranthub.com

Sketchbook

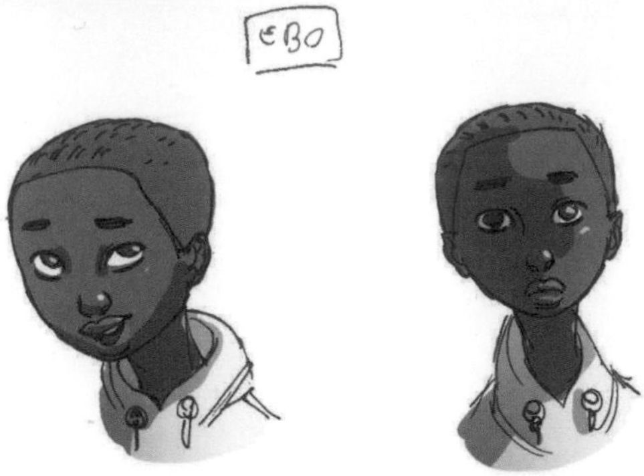
EBO

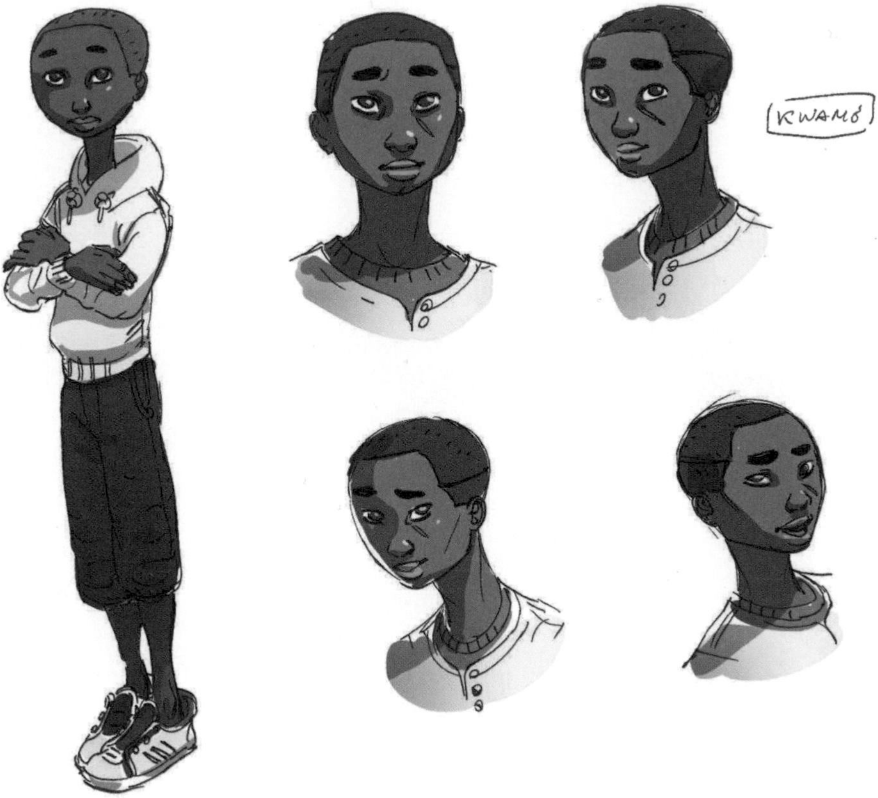
KWAME

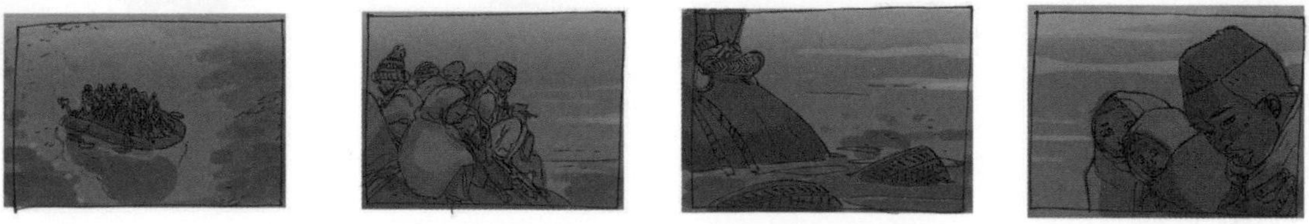

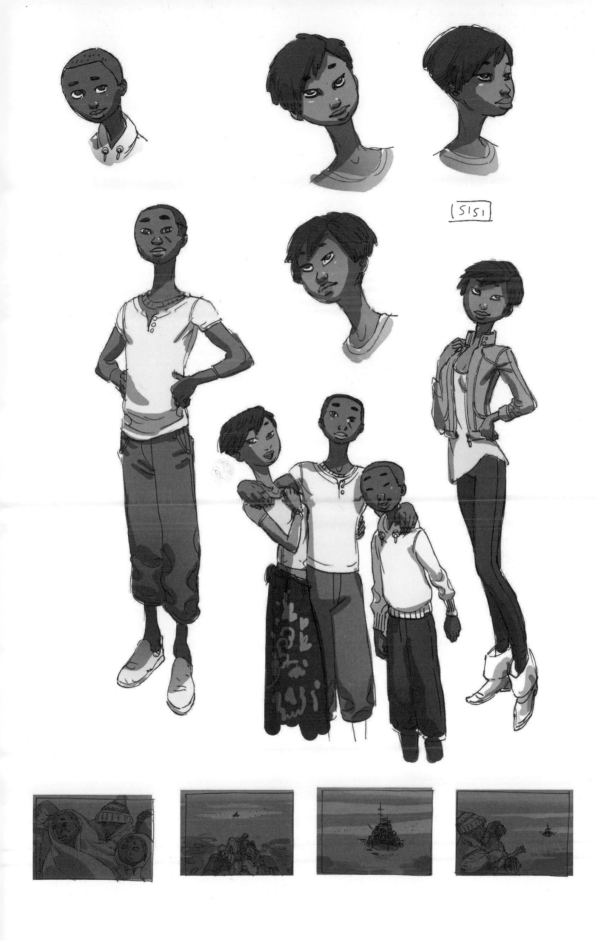

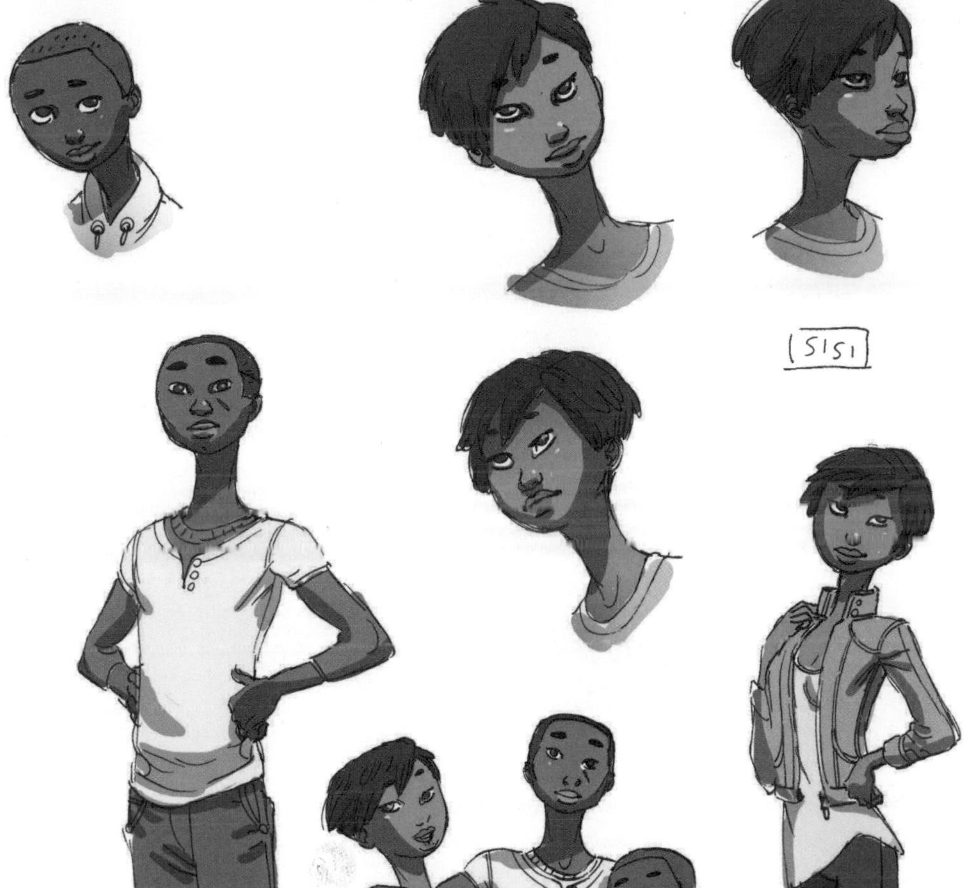
SISI

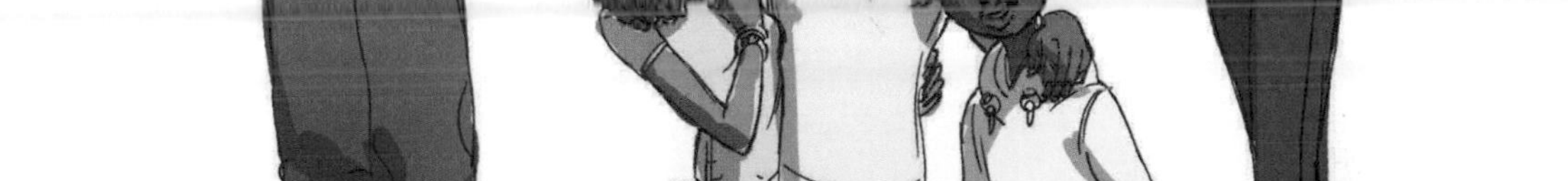

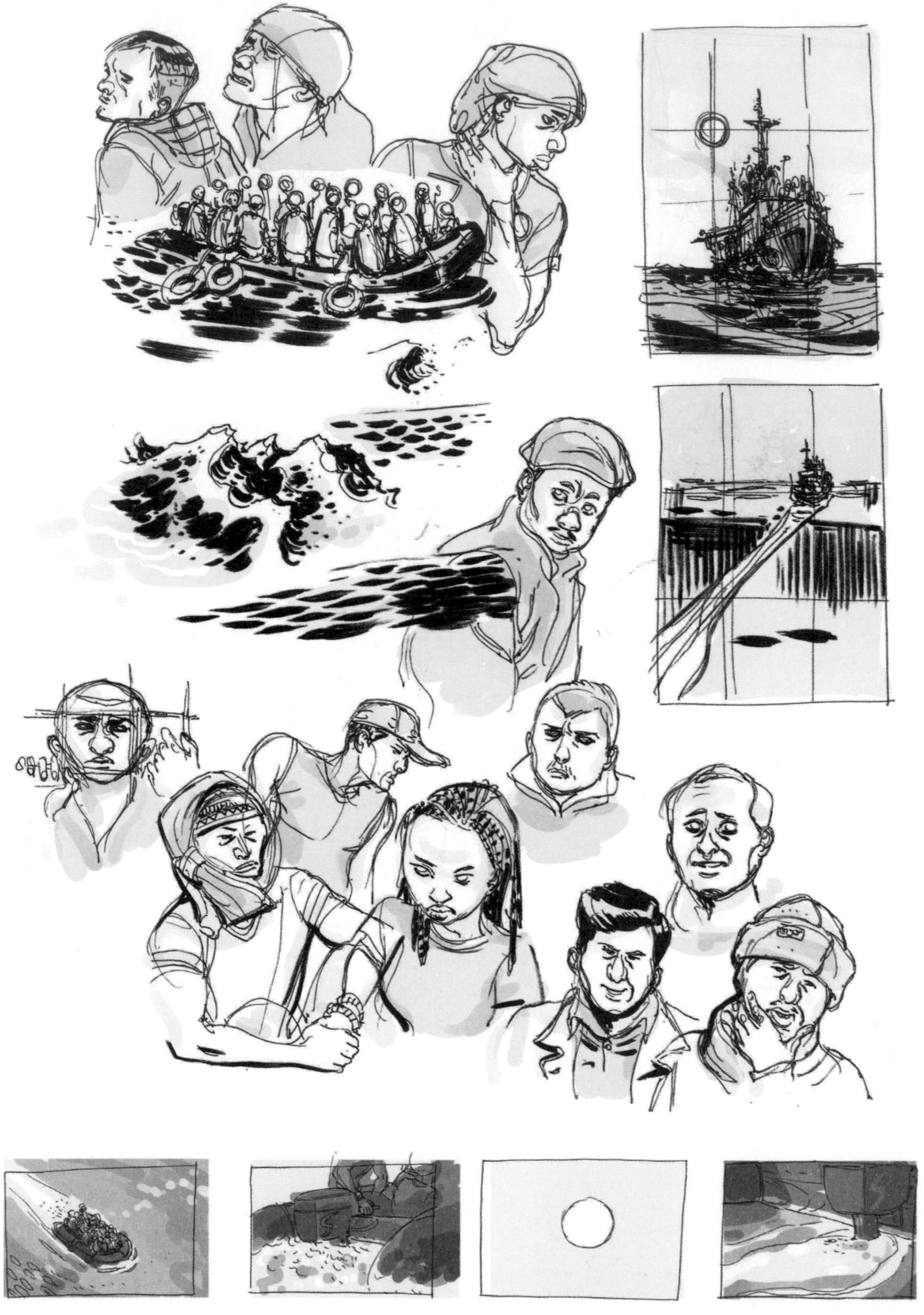

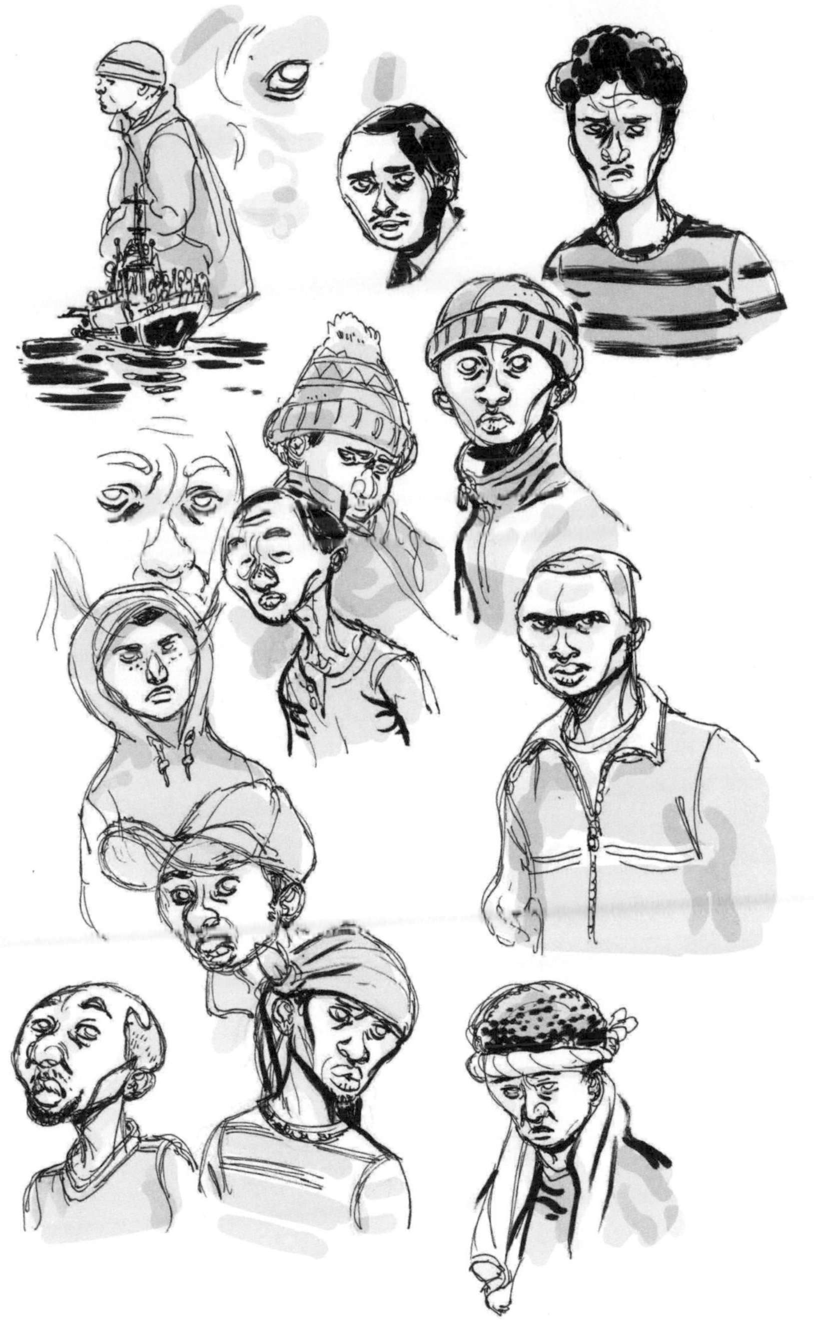

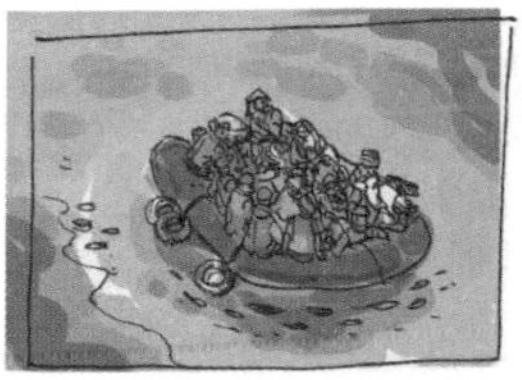

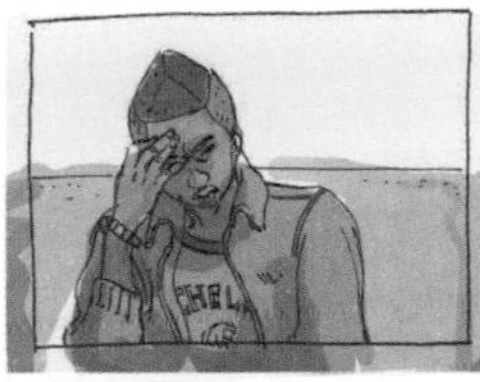

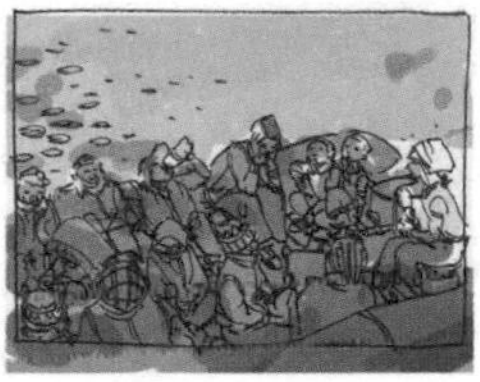

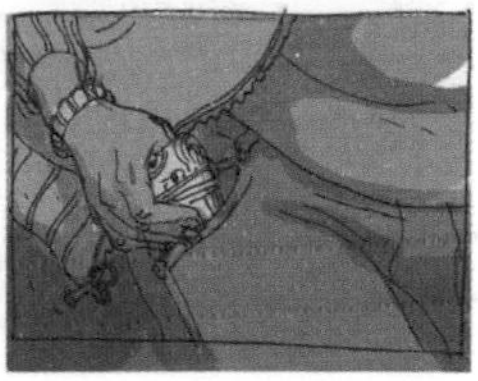

EOIN COLFER (pronounced Owen) was born in Wexford on the South-East coast of Ireland in 1965. He first developed an interest in writing when he was gripped by the Viking stories he learned about at school. After his marriage, he and his wife spent about four years working in Saudi Arabia, Tunisia, and Italy. His first book, *Benny and Omar*, was based on his experiences in Tunisia; it has since been translated into many languages. In 2001 the first Artemis Fowl book was published and Eoin gave up teaching to concentrate fully on writing. Eoin, who lives in Ireland with his wife and two children, says, "I will keep writing until people stop reading or I run out of ideas. Hopefully neither of these will happen anytime soon."

ANDREW DONKIN has sold over eight million children's books, graphic novels, and adult books. His work in comics includes *Batman: Legends of the Dark Knight* for DC Comics, and *Doctor Who*. With Eoin Colfer, he has co-written five bestselling graphic novel adaptations of Eoin's books. Andrew became interested in the issue of migrants and asylum while writing the biography of Sir Alfred Mehran, a stateless man who lived on a bench in Paris Airport for eighteen years. The resulting book, *The Terminal Man*, was described by *The Sunday Times* (Glasgow) as "a brilliant and profoundly disturbing book." Andrew lives near the river Thames in London with his family.

GIOVANNI RIGANO is an Italian comics artist and creator of many graphic novels. He has adapted five of Eoin Colfer's novels into graphic novels, as well as Disney-Pixar's *The Incredibles*, three *Pirates of the Caribbean* novels, and his own series, *Daffodil*. He lives in Como, Italy.